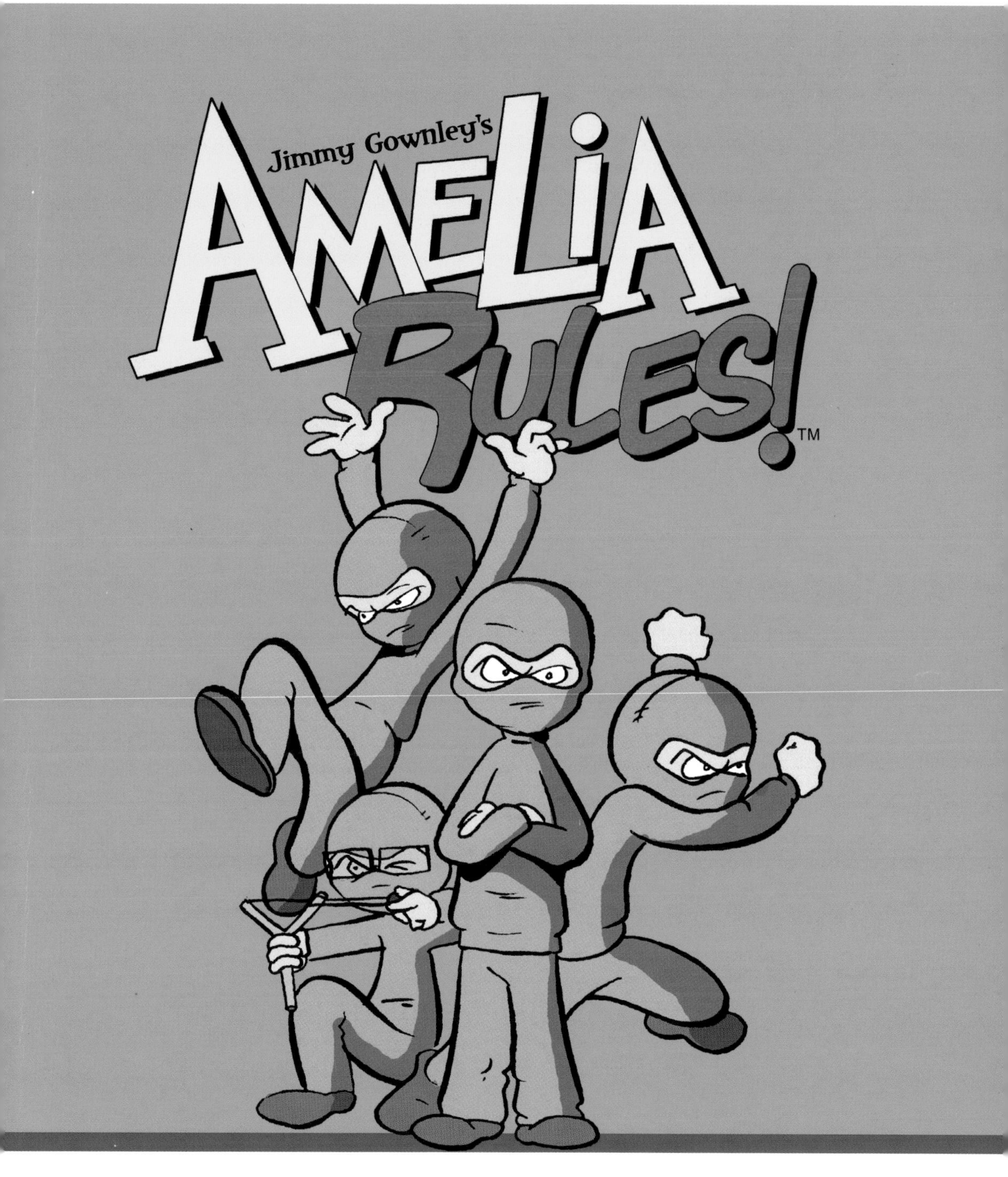
Jimmy Gownley's
AMELIA RULES!™

Her Three Kisses

Atheneum Books for Young Readers
New York London Toronto Sydney

Spotlight

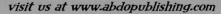

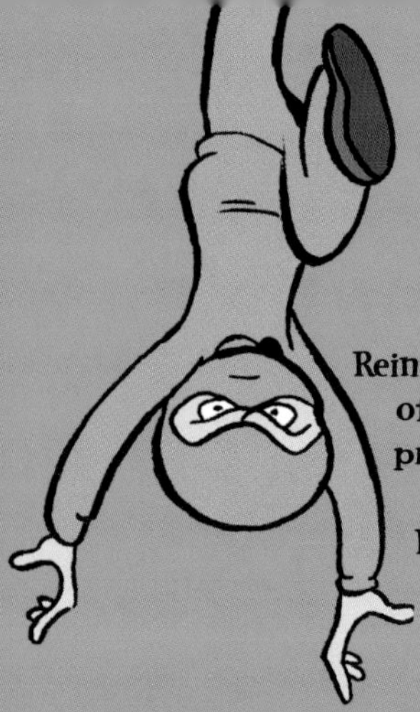

visit us at www.abdopublishing.com

Reinforced library bound edition published in 2013 by Spotlight, a division of the ABDO Group, PO Box 398166, Minneapolis, MN 55439. Spotlight produces high-quality reinforced library bound editions for schools and libraries. Published by agreement with Atheneum Books for Young Readers, an imprint of Simon & Schuster Children's Publishing Division.

Printed in the United States of America, North Mankato, Minnesota.
102012
012013
This book contains at least 10% recycled materials.

· Special thanks to Michael Cohen ·

This book is a work of fiction. Any references to historical events, real people, or real locales are used fictitiously. Other names, characters, places, and incidents are products of the author's imagination, and any resemblance to actual events or locales or persons, living or dead, is entirely coincidental.

Book design by Jimmy Gownley and Sonia Chaghatzbanian

Library of Congress Cataloging-in-Publication Data

Gownley, Jimmy.
Amelia and her three kisses / [Jimmy Gownley]. -- Reinforced library bound ed.
p. cm. -- (Jimmy Gownley's Amelia rules!)
Summary: After the funeral of a great-aunt she never met, Amelia McBride is pressured into joining a game of spin-the-bottle with "the ninjas," who turn out to be the sons of Aunt Tanner's childhood enemy, Julie.
ISBN 978-1-61479-068-6
[1. Graphic novels. 2. Kissing--Fiction. 3. Peer pressure--Fiction. 4. Aunts--Fiction. 5. Family life--Fiction. 6. Funeral rites and ceremonies--Fiction.] I. Title.
PZ7.7.G69Akm 2013
741.5'973--dc23

2012026900

Spotlight

All Spotlight books are reinforced library bindings
and manufactured in the United States of America.

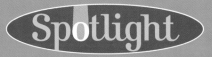

To my beautiful girls:
Stella Mary and
Anna Elizabeth,
And to their wonderful mother, Karen.

You're what make ME happy.

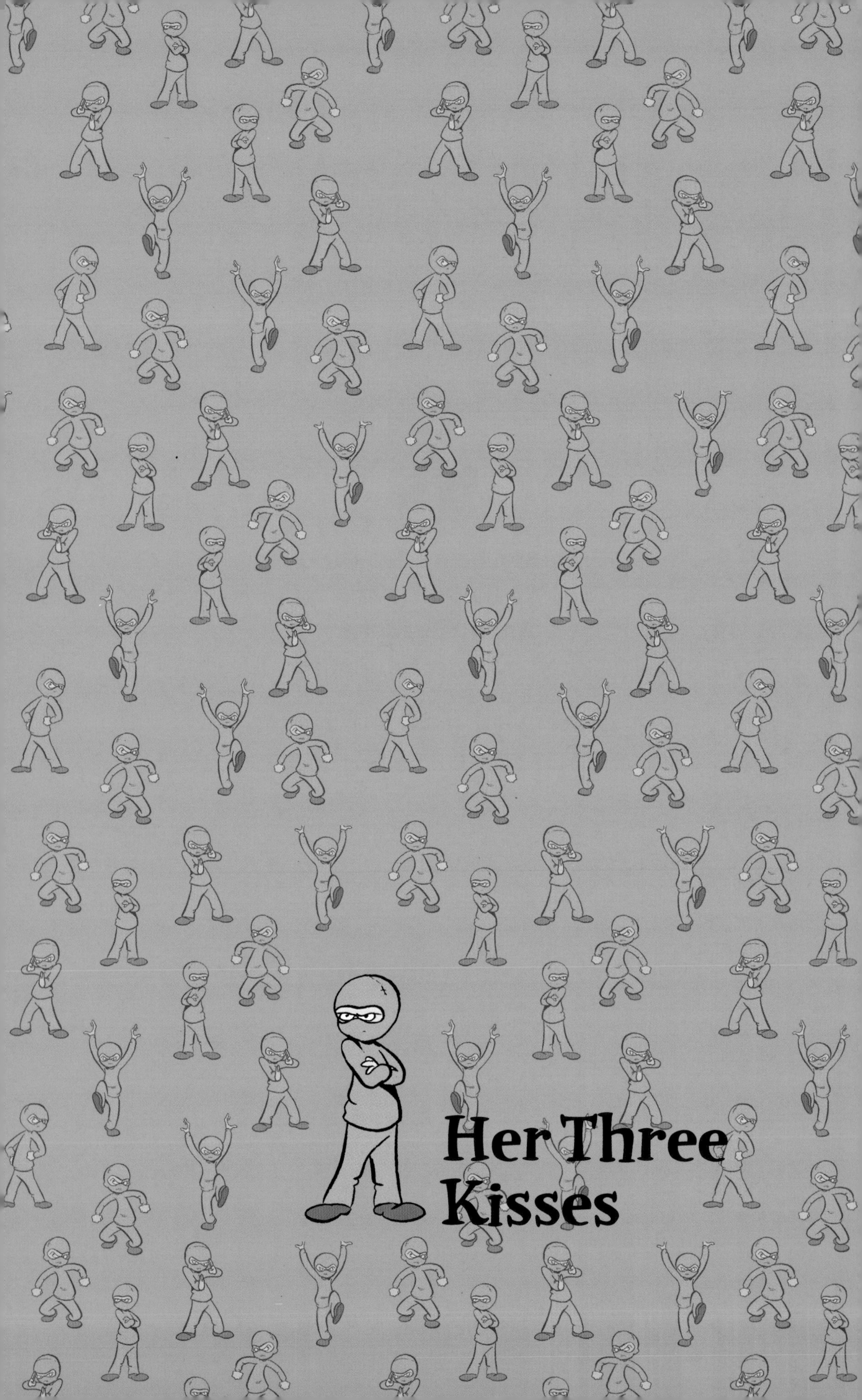
Her Three
Kisses

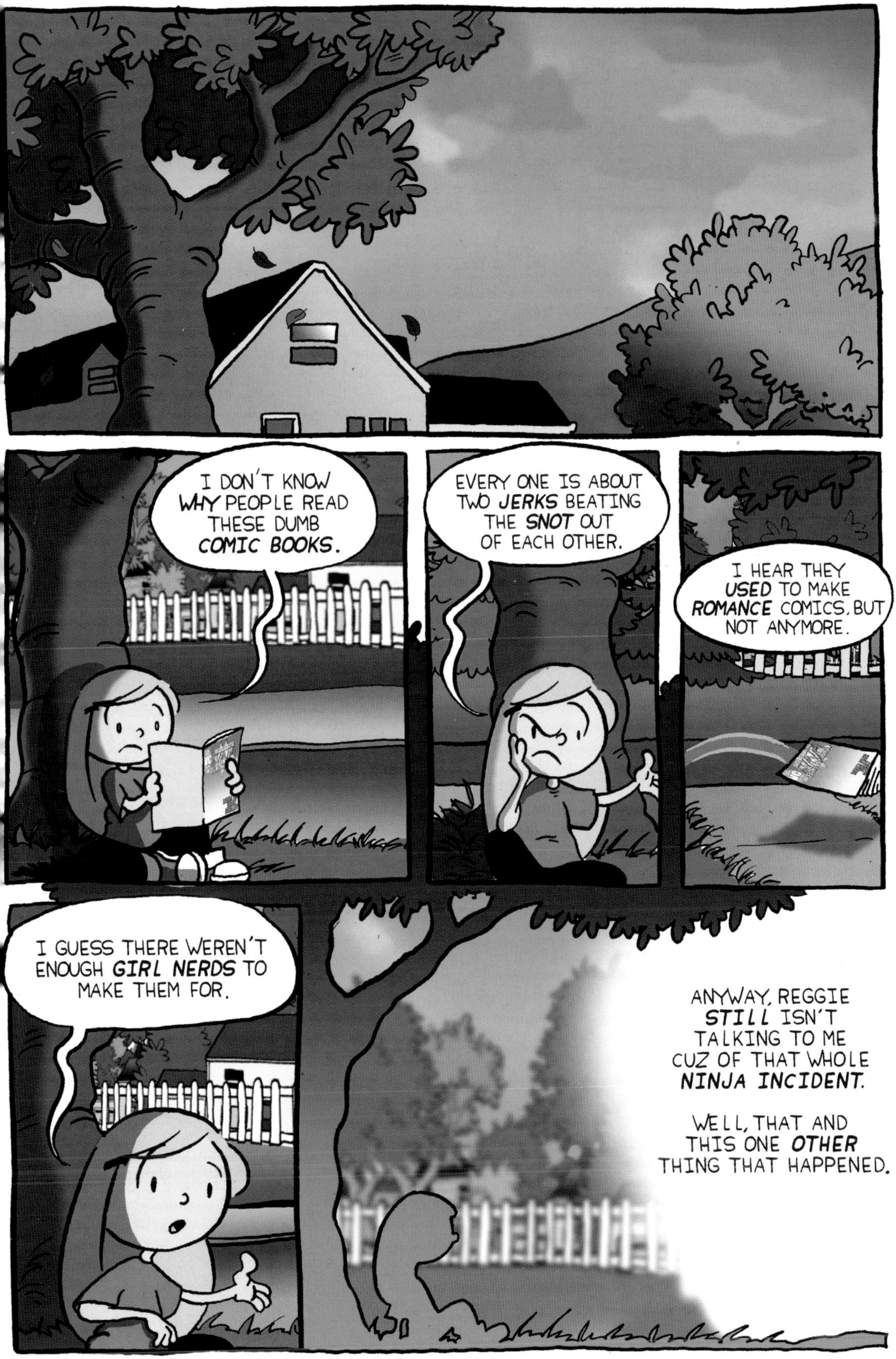

I DON'T KNOW WHY PEOPLE READ THESE DUMB COMIC BOOKS.
EVERY ONE IS ABOUT TWO JERKS BEATING THE SNOT OUT OF EACH OTHER.
I HEAR THEY USED TO MAKE ROMANCE COMICS, BUT NOT ANYMORE.
I GUESS THERE WEREN'T ENOUGH GIRL NERDS TO MAKE THEM FOR.
ANYWAY, REGGIE STILL ISN'T TALKING TO ME CUZ OF THAT WHOLE NINJA INCIDENT.
WELL, THAT AND THIS ONE OTHER THING THAT HAPPENED.

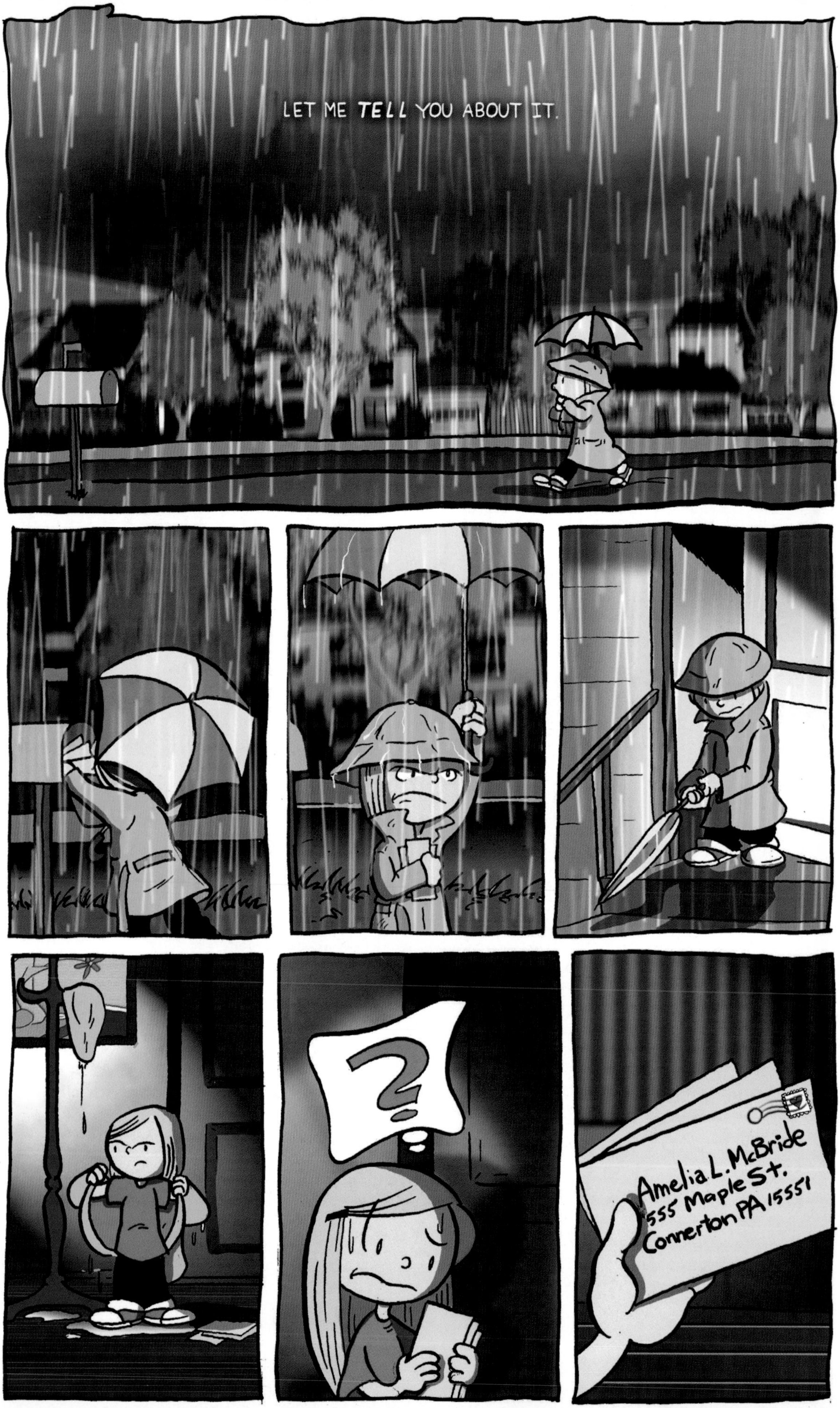
LET ME TELL YOU ABOUT IT.
?
Amelia L. McBride
555 Maple St.
Connerton PA 15551

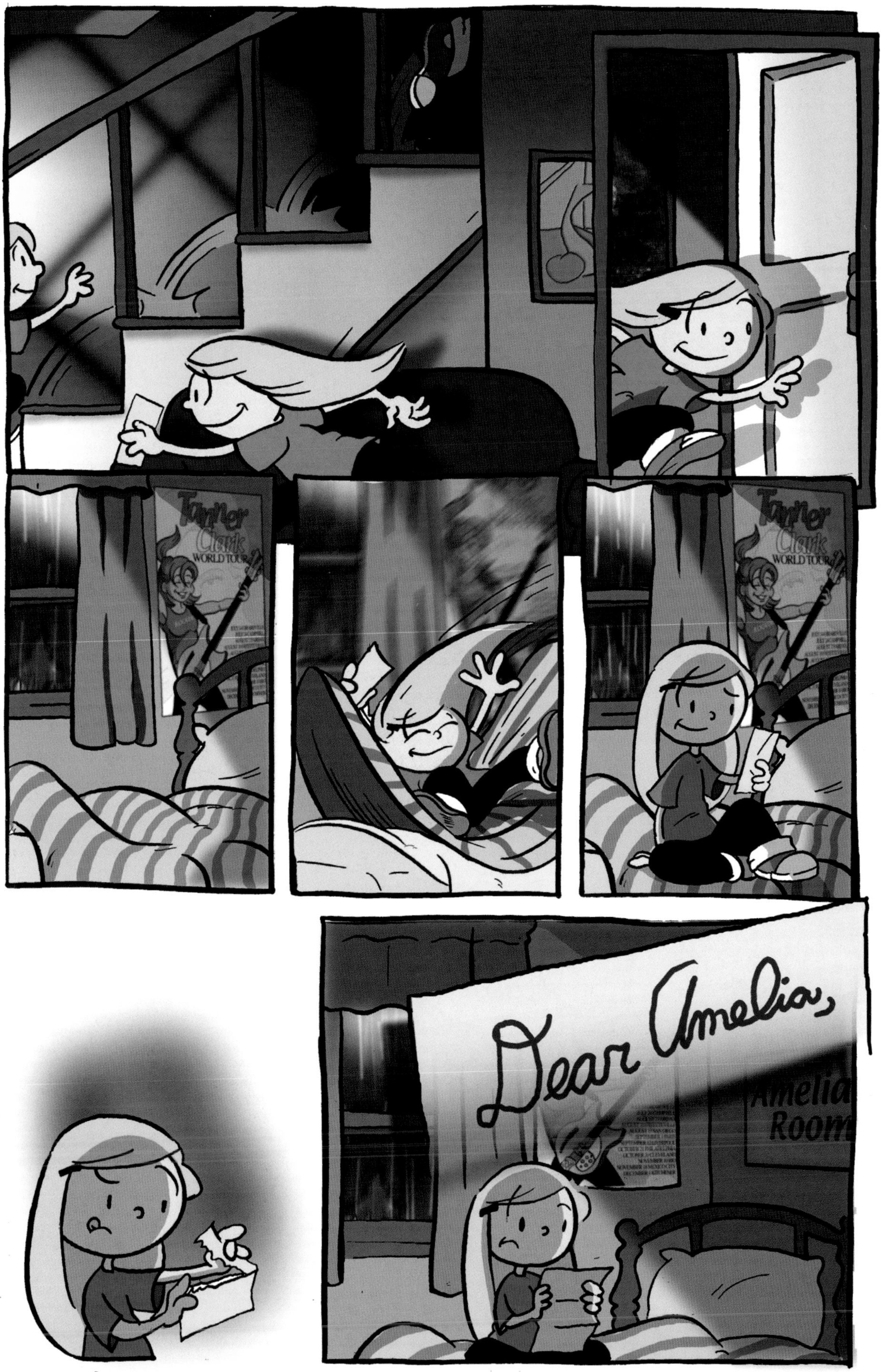

Tanner Clark
WORLD TOUR
Dear Amelia,
Amelia
Room

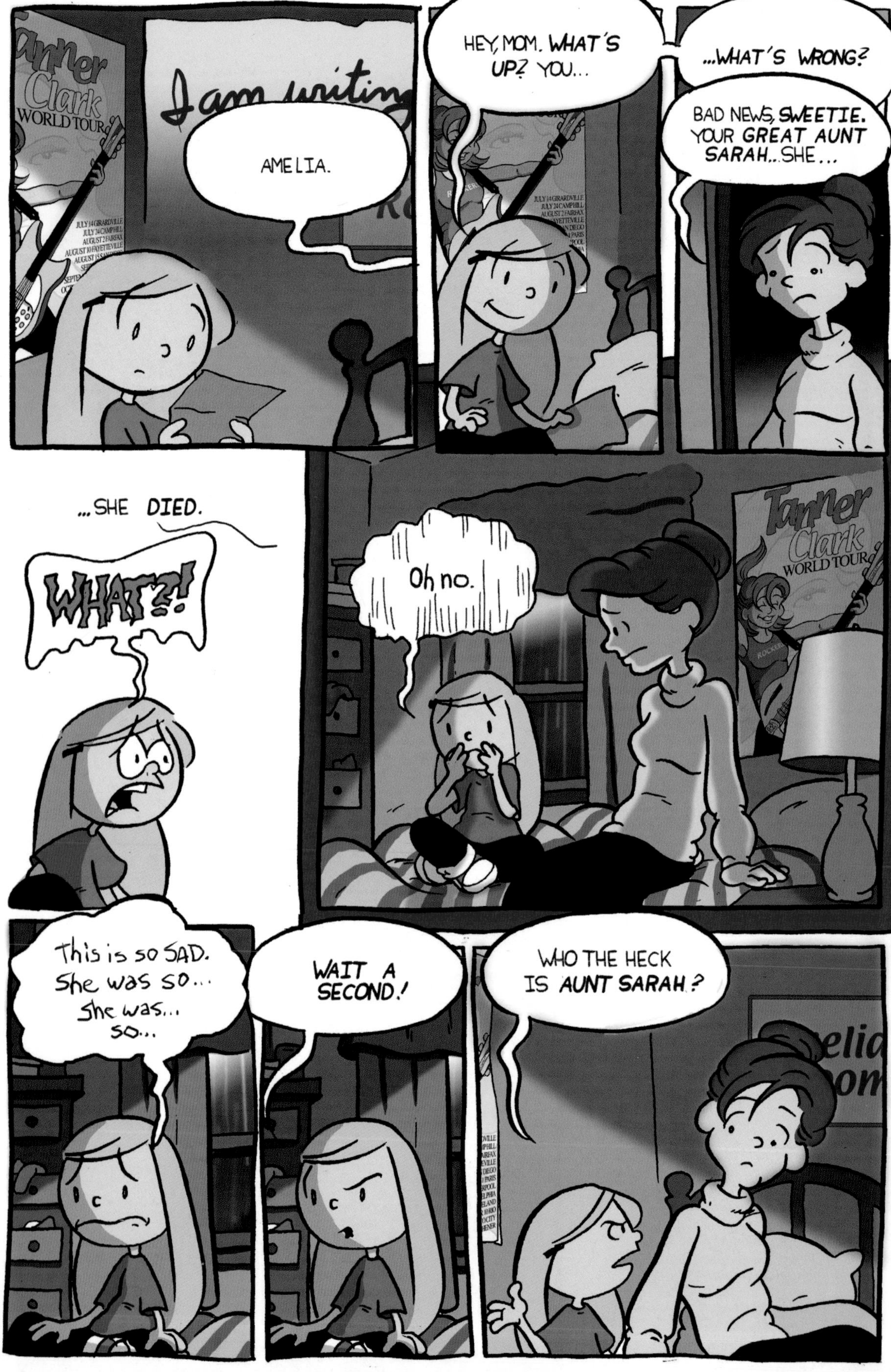
Tanner Clark
WORLD TOUR
I am writing
AMELIA.
HEY, MOM. WHAT'S UP? YOU...
...WHAT'S WRONG?
BAD NEWS, SWEETIE. YOUR GREAT AUNT SARAH... SHE...
...SHE DIED.
WHAT?!
Tanner Clark
WORLD TOUR
Oh no.
This is so SAD. She was so... She was... so...
WAIT A SECOND!
WHO THE HECK IS AUNT SARAH?

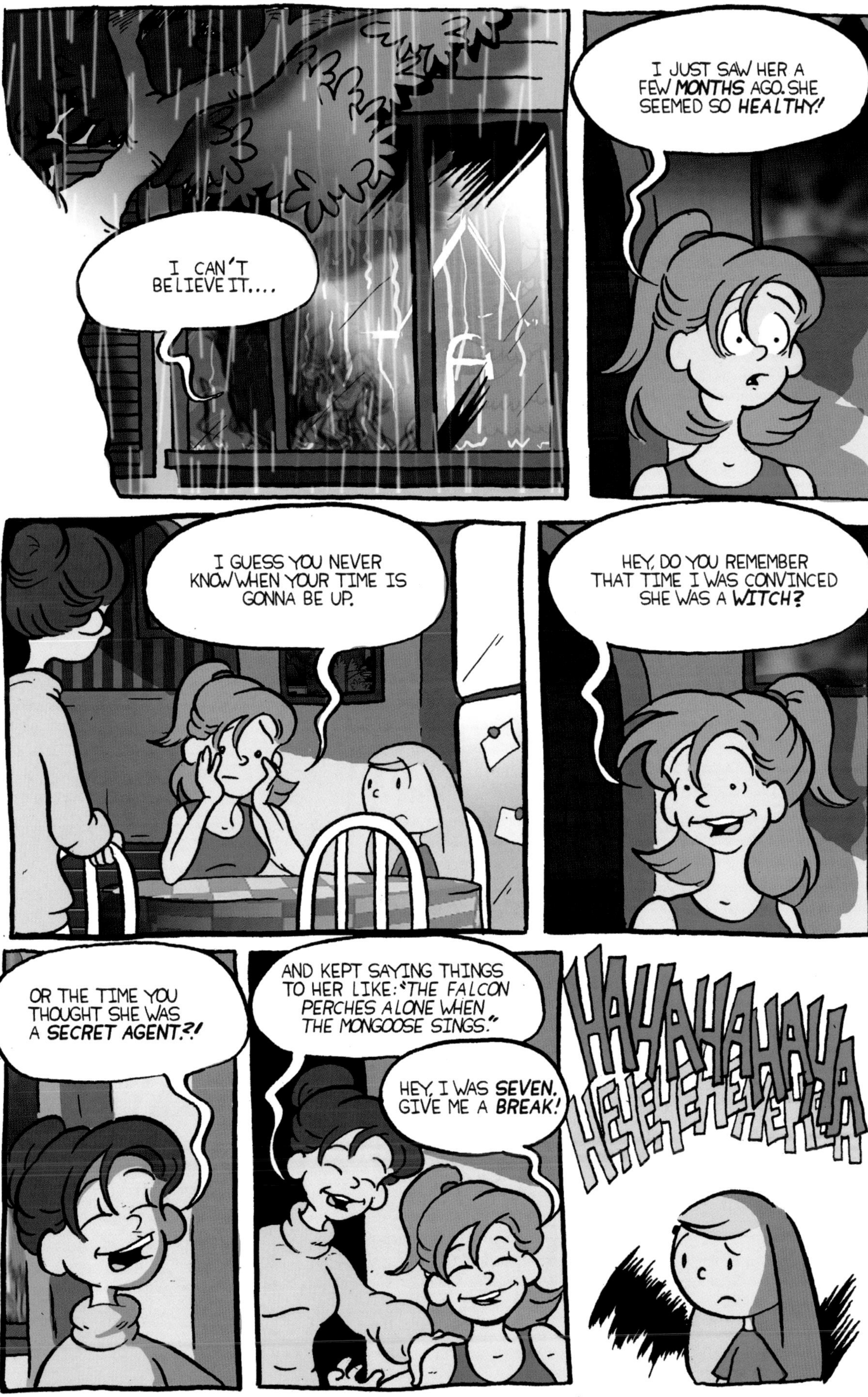
I CAN'T BELIEVE IT....
I JUST SAW HER A FEW MONTHS AGO. SHE SEEMED SO HEALTHY!
I GUESS YOU NEVER KNOW WHEN YOUR TIME IS GONNA BE UP.
HEY, DO YOU REMEMBER THAT TIME I WAS CONVINCED SHE WAS A WITCH?
OR THE TIME YOU THOUGHT SHE WAS A SECRET AGENT?!
AND KEPT SAYING THINGS TO HER LIKE: "THE FALCON PERCHES ALONE WHEN THE MONGOOSE SINGS."
HEY, I WAS SEVEN. GIVE ME A BREAK!
HAHAHAHAHAHA
HEHEHEHEHEHEHEHA

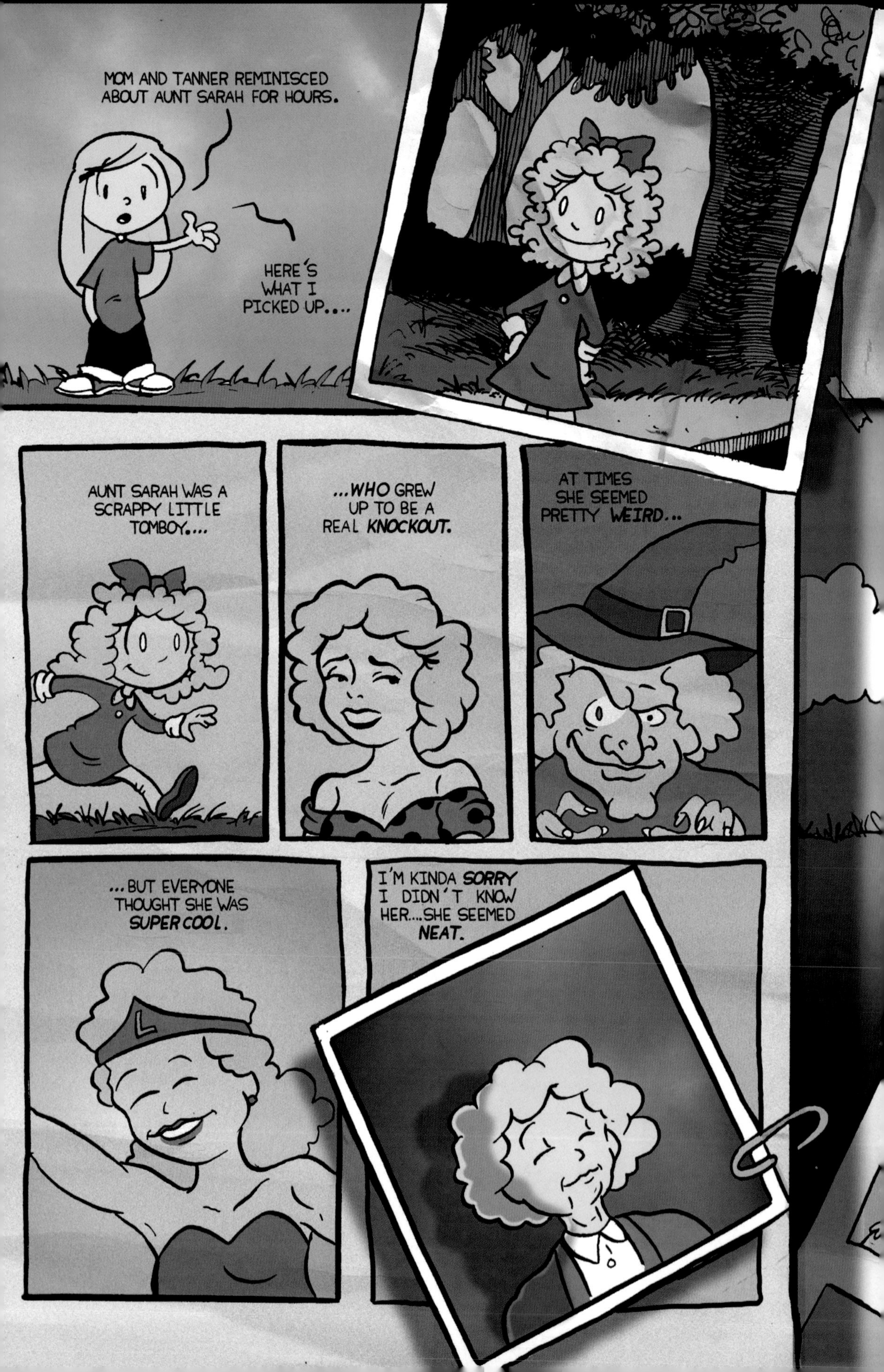
MOM AND TANNER REMINISCED ABOUT AUNT SARAH FOR HOURS.
HERE'S WHAT I PICKED UP....
AUNT SARAH WAS A SCRAPPY LITTLE TOMBOY....
...WHO GREW UP TO BE A REAL KNOCKOUT.
AT TIMES SHE SEEMED PRETTY WEIRD...
...BUT EVERYONE THOUGHT SHE WAS SUPER COOL.
I'M KINDA SORRY I DIDN'T KNOW HER....SHE SEEMED NEAT.

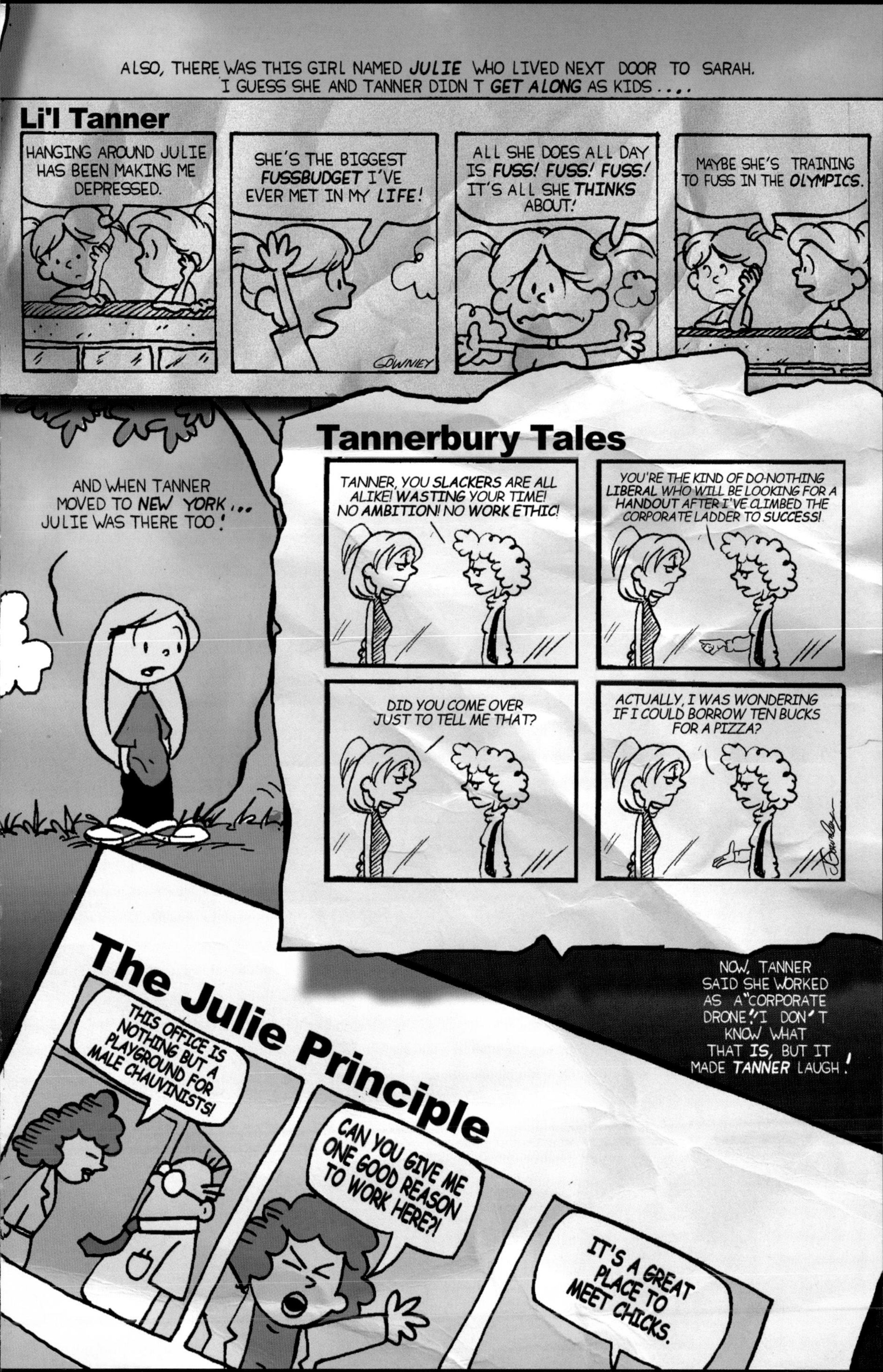

ALSO, THERE WAS THIS GIRL NAMED JULIE WHO LIVED NEXT DOOR TO SARAH. I GUESS SHE AND TANNER DIDN'T GET ALONG AS KIDS....
Li'l Tanner
HANGING AROUND JULIE HAS BEEN MAKING ME DEPRESSED.
SHE'S THE BIGGEST FUSSBUDGET I'VE EVER MET IN MY LIFE!
ALL SHE DOES ALL DAY IS FUSS! FUSS! FUSS! IT'S ALL SHE THINKS ABOUT!
MAYBE SHE'S TRAINING TO FUSS IN THE OLYMPICS.
GOWNLEY
AND WHEN TANNER MOVED TO NEW YORK... JULIE WAS THERE TOO!
Tannerbury Tales
TANNER, YOU SLACKERS ARE ALL ALIKE! WASTING YOUR TIME! NO AMBITION! NO WORK ETHIC!
YOU'RE THE KIND OF DO-NOTHING LIBERAL WHO WILL BE LOOKING FOR A HANDOUT AFTER I'VE CLIMBED THE CORPORATE LADDER TO SUCCESS!
DID YOU COME OVER JUST TO TELL ME THAT?
ACTUALLY, I WAS WONDERING IF I COULD BORROW TEN BUCKS FOR A PIZZA?
NOW, TANNER SAID SHE WORKED AS A "CORPORATE DRONE." I DON'T KNOW WHAT THAT IS, BUT IT MADE TANNER LAUGH!
The Julie Principle
THIS OFFICE IS NOTHING BUT A PLAYGROUND FOR MALE CHAUVINISTS!
CAN YOU GIVE ME ONE GOOD REASON TO WORK HERE?!
IT'S A GREAT PLACE TO MEET CHICKS.

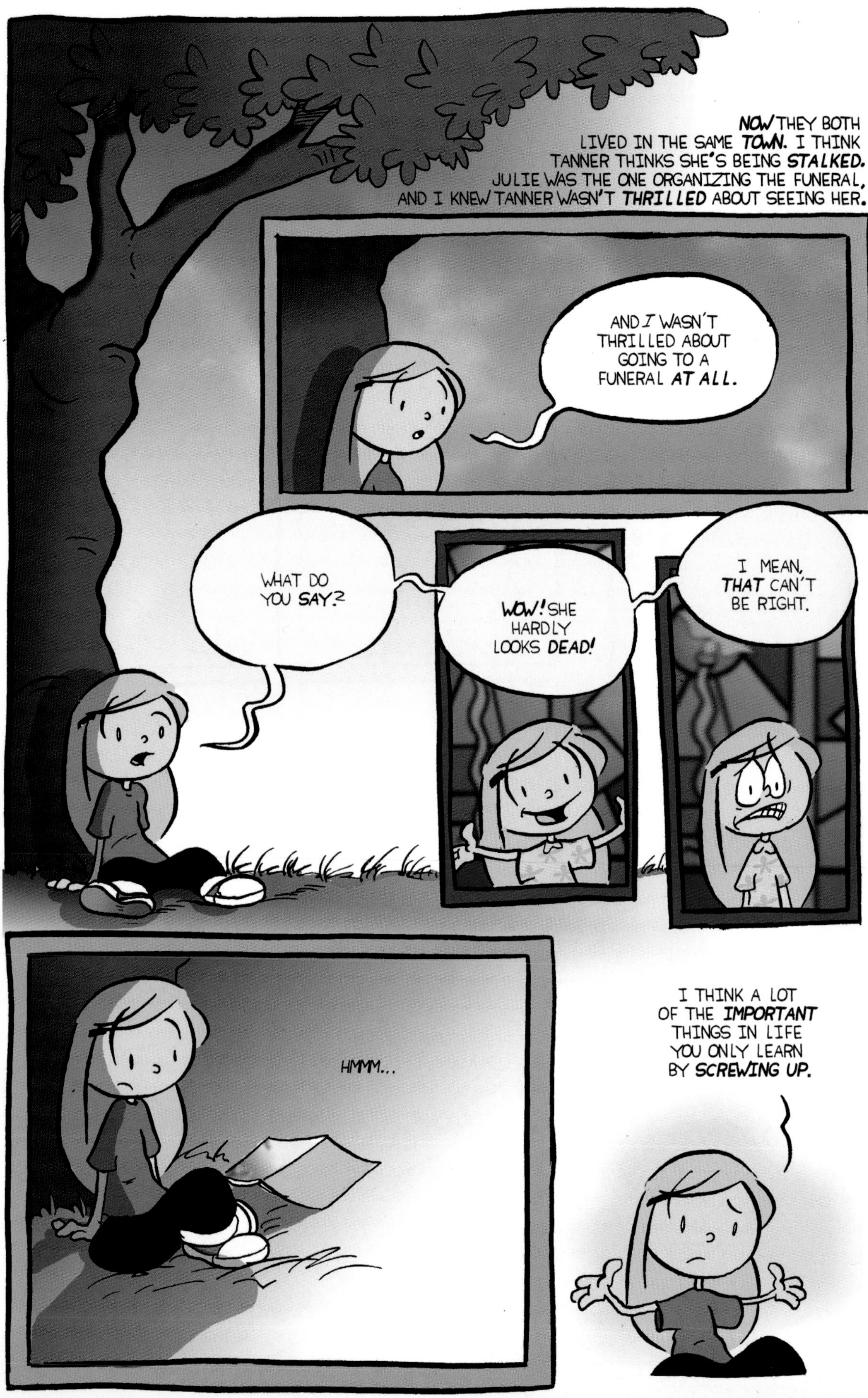
NOW THEY BOTH LIVED IN THE SAME TOWN. I THINK TANNER THINKS SHE'S BEING STALKED. JULIE WAS THE ONE ORGANIZING THE FUNERAL, AND I KNEW TANNER WASN'T THRILLED ABOUT SEEING HER.
AND I WASN'T THRILLED ABOUT GOING TO A FUNERAL AT ALL.
WHAT DO YOU SAY?
WOW! SHE HARDLY LOOKS DEAD!
I MEAN, THAT CAN'T BE RIGHT.
HMMM...
I THINK A LOT OF THE IMPORTANT THINGS IN LIFE YOU ONLY LEARN BY SCREWING UP.

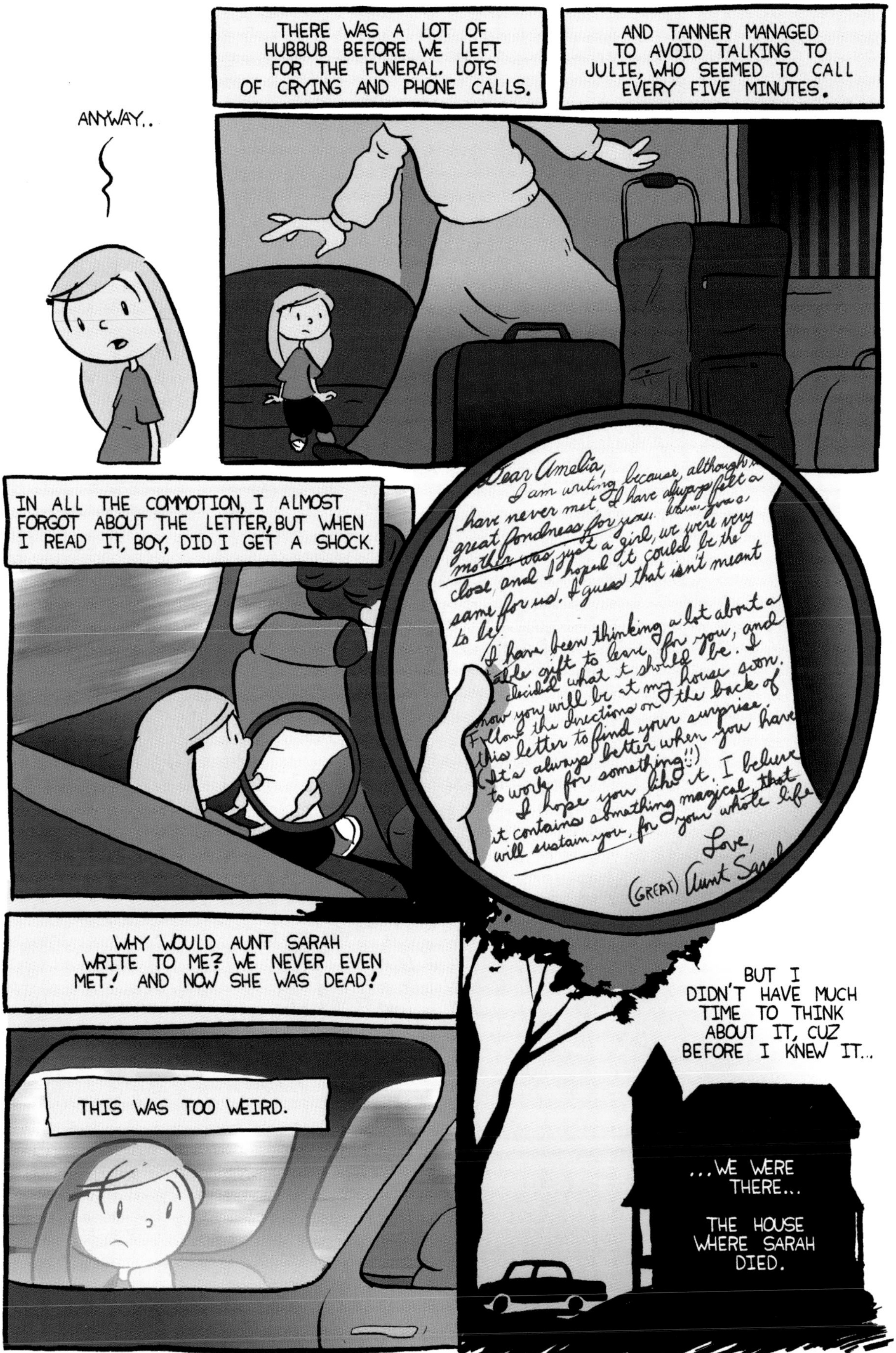
THERE WAS A LOT OF HUBBUB BEFORE WE LEFT FOR THE FUNERAL. LOTS OF CRYING AND PHONE CALLS.
AND TANNER MANAGED TO AVOID TALKING TO JULIE, WHO SEEMED TO CALL EVERY FIVE MINUTES.
ANYWAY..
IN ALL THE COMMOTION, I ALMOST FORGOT ABOUT THE LETTER, BUT WHEN I READ IT, BOY, DID I GET A SHOCK.
Dear Amelia,
I am writing because, although
have never met, I have always felt a
great fondness for you. When your
mother was just a girl, we were very
close, and I hoped it could be the
same for us. I guess that isn't meant
to be.
I have been thinking a lot about a
table gift to leave for you, and
decided what it should be. I
now you will be at my house soon.
Follow the directions on the back of
this letter to find your surprise.
(It's always better when you have
to work for something!!)
I hope you like it. I believe
it contains something magical that
will sustain you, for your whole life.
Love,
(GREAT) Aunt Sar
WHY WOULD AUNT SARAH WRITE TO ME? WE NEVER EVEN MET! AND NOW SHE WAS DEAD!
THIS WAS TOO WEIRD.
BUT I DIDN'T HAVE MUCH TIME TO THINK ABOUT IT, CUZ BEFORE I KNEW IT...
...WE WERE THERE...
THE HOUSE WHERE SARAH DIED.

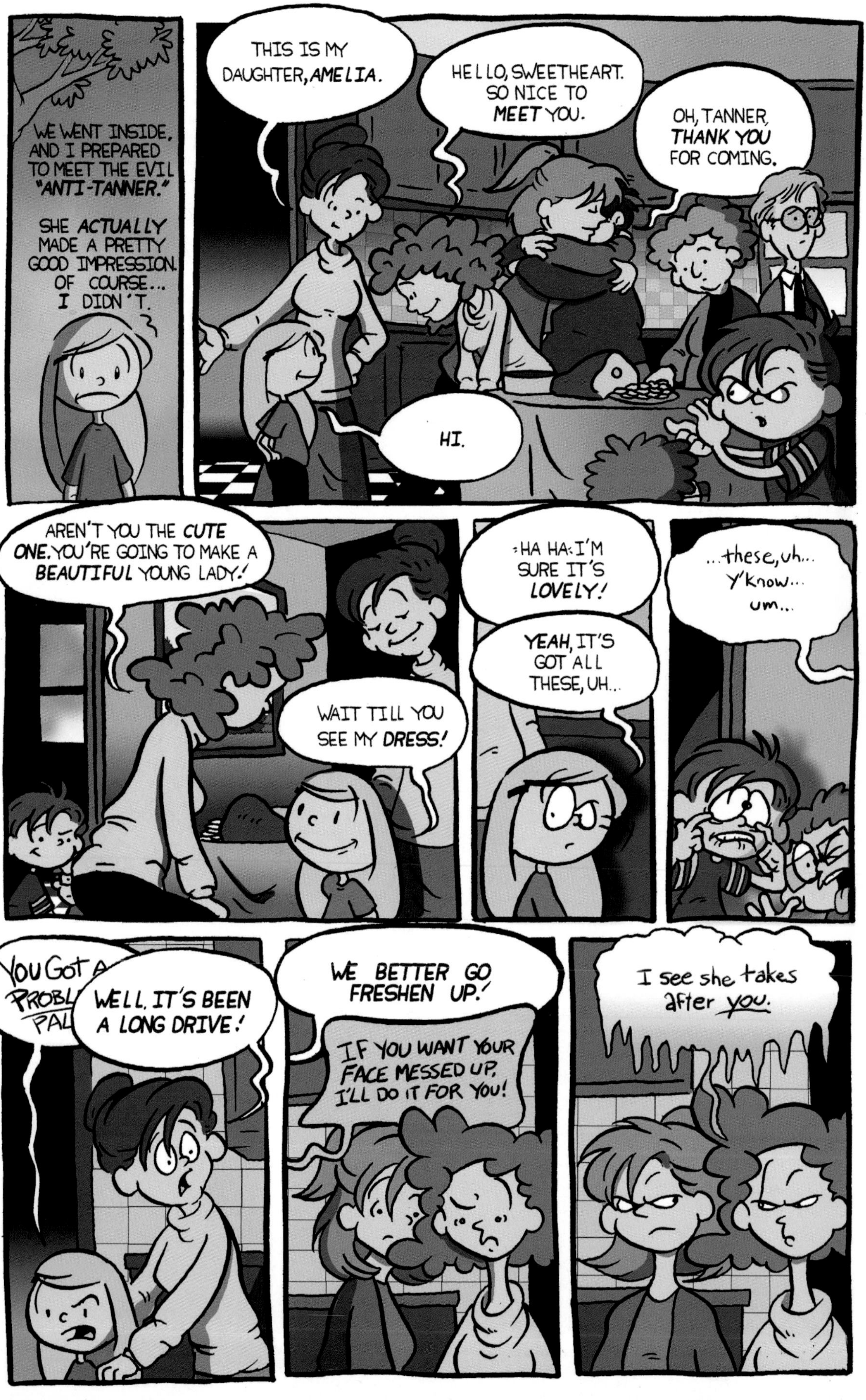
WE WENT INSIDE, AND I PREPARED TO MEET THE EVIL "ANTI-TANNER."
SHE ACTUALLY MADE A PRETTY GOOD IMPRESSION. OF COURSE... I DIDN'T.
THIS IS MY DAUGHTER, AMELIA.
HELLO, SWEETHEART. SO NICE TO MEET YOU.
OH, TANNER, THANK YOU FOR COMING.
HI.
AREN'T YOU THE CUTE ONE. YOU'RE GOING TO MAKE A BEAUTIFUL YOUNG LADY!
WAIT TILL YOU SEE MY DRESS!
HA HA I'M SURE IT'S LOVELY!
YEAH, IT'S GOT ALL THESE, UH...
...these, uh... y'know... um...
You Got A PROBL PAL
WELL, IT'S BEEN A LONG DRIVE!
WE BETTER GO FRESHEN UP.
IF YOU WANT YOUR FACE MESSED UP, I'LL DO IT FOR YOU!
I see she takes after you.

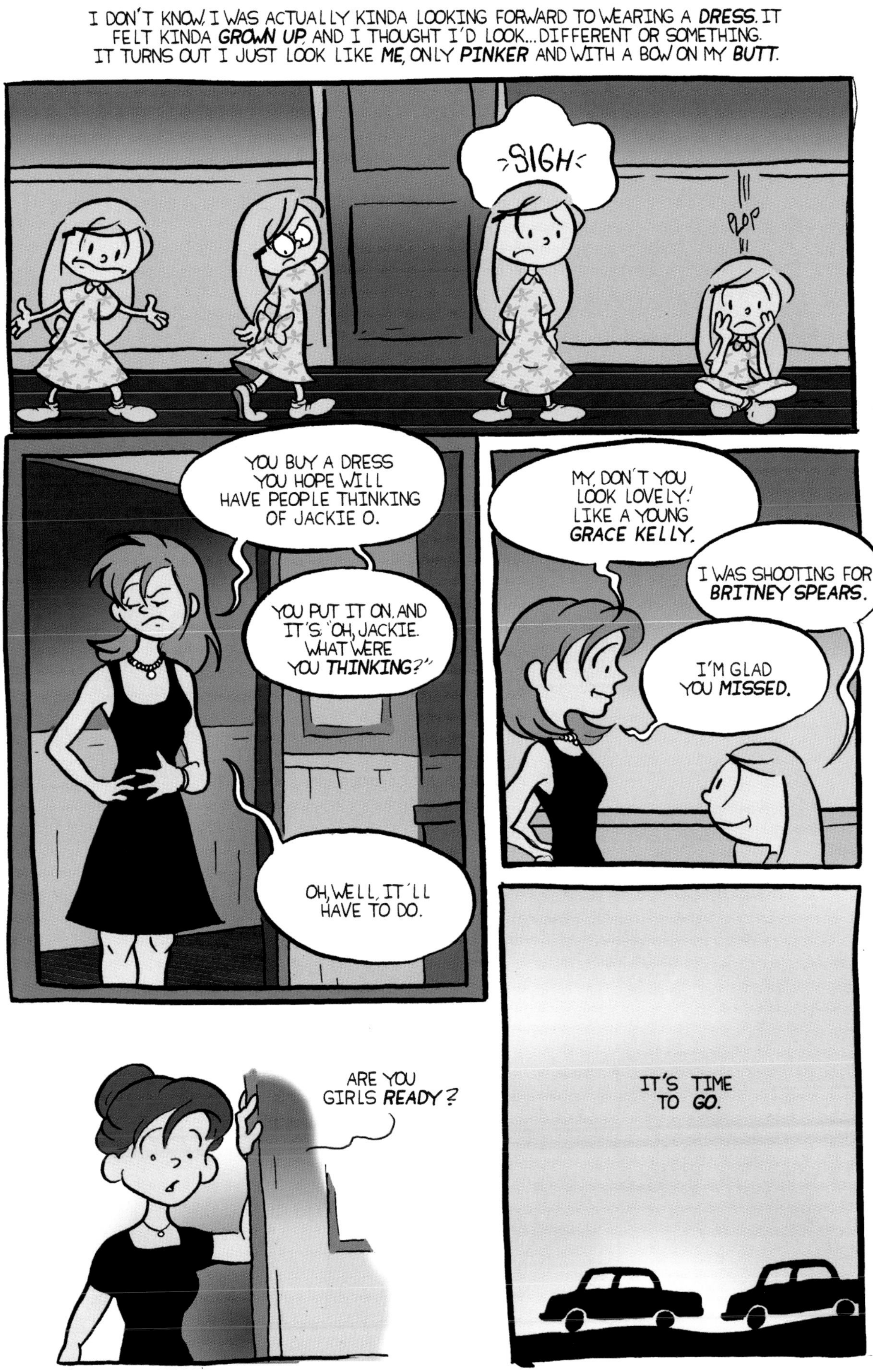
I DON'T KNOW, I WAS ACTUALLY KINDA LOOKING FORWARD TO WEARING A **DRESS**. IT FELT KINDA **GROWN UP**, AND I THOUGHT I'D LOOK... DIFFERENT OR SOMETHING. IT TURNS OUT I JUST LOOK LIKE **ME**, ONLY **PINKER** AND WITH A BOW ON MY **BUTT**.
SIGH
PLOP
YOU BUY A DRESS YOU HOPE WILL HAVE PEOPLE THINKING OF JACKIE O.
YOU PUT IT ON, AND IT'S: "OH, JACKIE. WHAT WERE YOU **THINKING**?"
OH, WELL, IT'LL HAVE TO DO.
MY, DON'T YOU LOOK LOVELY! LIKE A YOUNG **GRACE KELLY**.
I WAS SHOOTING FOR **BRITNEY SPEARS**.
I'M GLAD YOU **MISSED**.
ARE YOU GIRLS **READY**?
IT'S TIME TO **GO**.

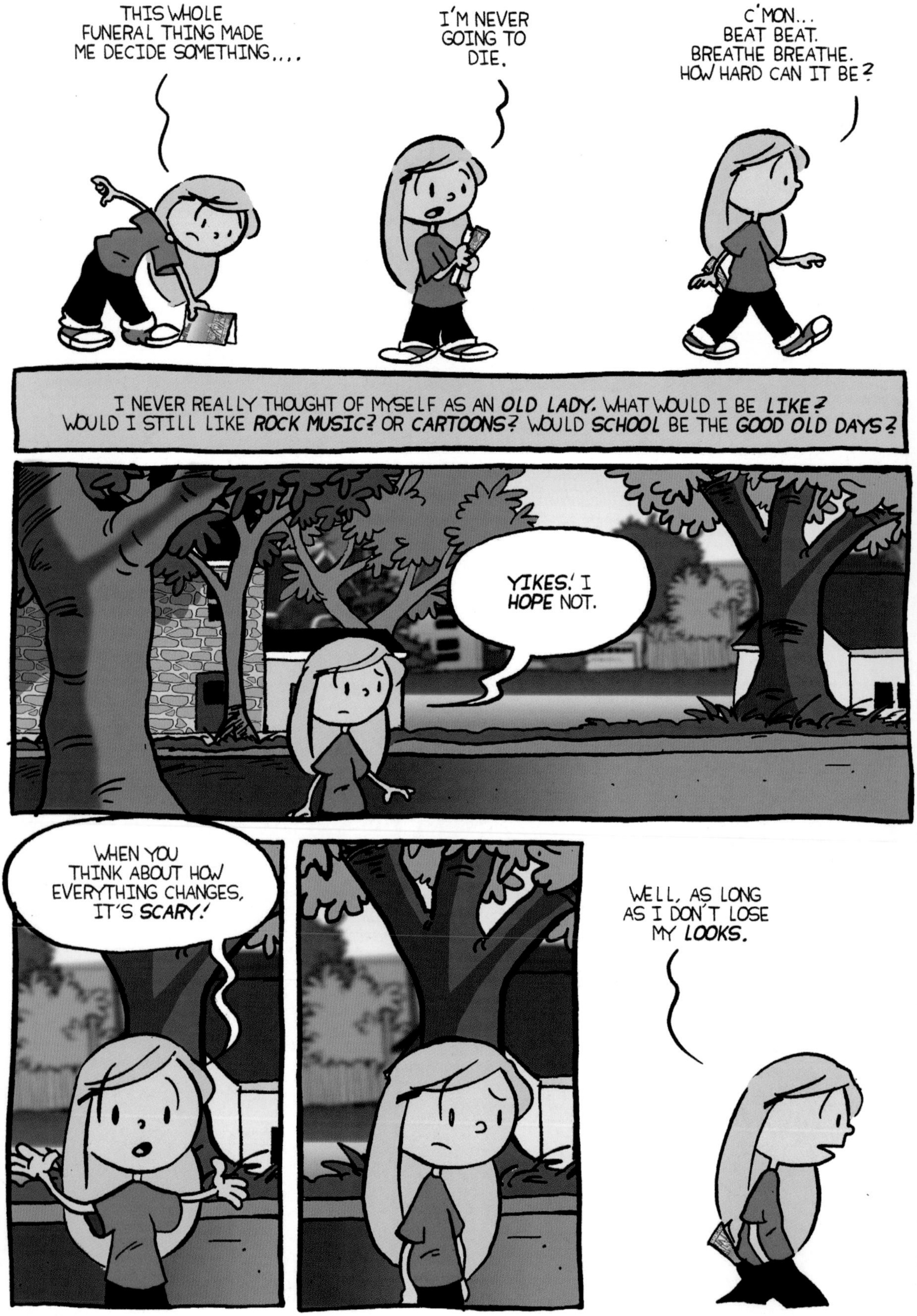
THIS WHOLE FUNERAL THING MADE ME DECIDE SOMETHING....
I'M NEVER GOING TO DIE.
C'MON... BEAT BEAT. BREATHE BREATHE. HOW HARD CAN IT BE?
I NEVER REALLY THOUGHT OF MYSELF AS AN OLD LADY. WHAT WOULD I BE LIKE? WOULD I STILL LIKE ROCK MUSIC? OR CARTOONS? WOULD SCHOOL BE THE GOOD OLD DAYS?
YIKES! I HOPE NOT.
WHEN YOU THINK ABOUT HOW EVERYTHING CHANGES, IT'S SCARY!
WELL, AS LONG AS I DON'T LOSE MY LOOKS.

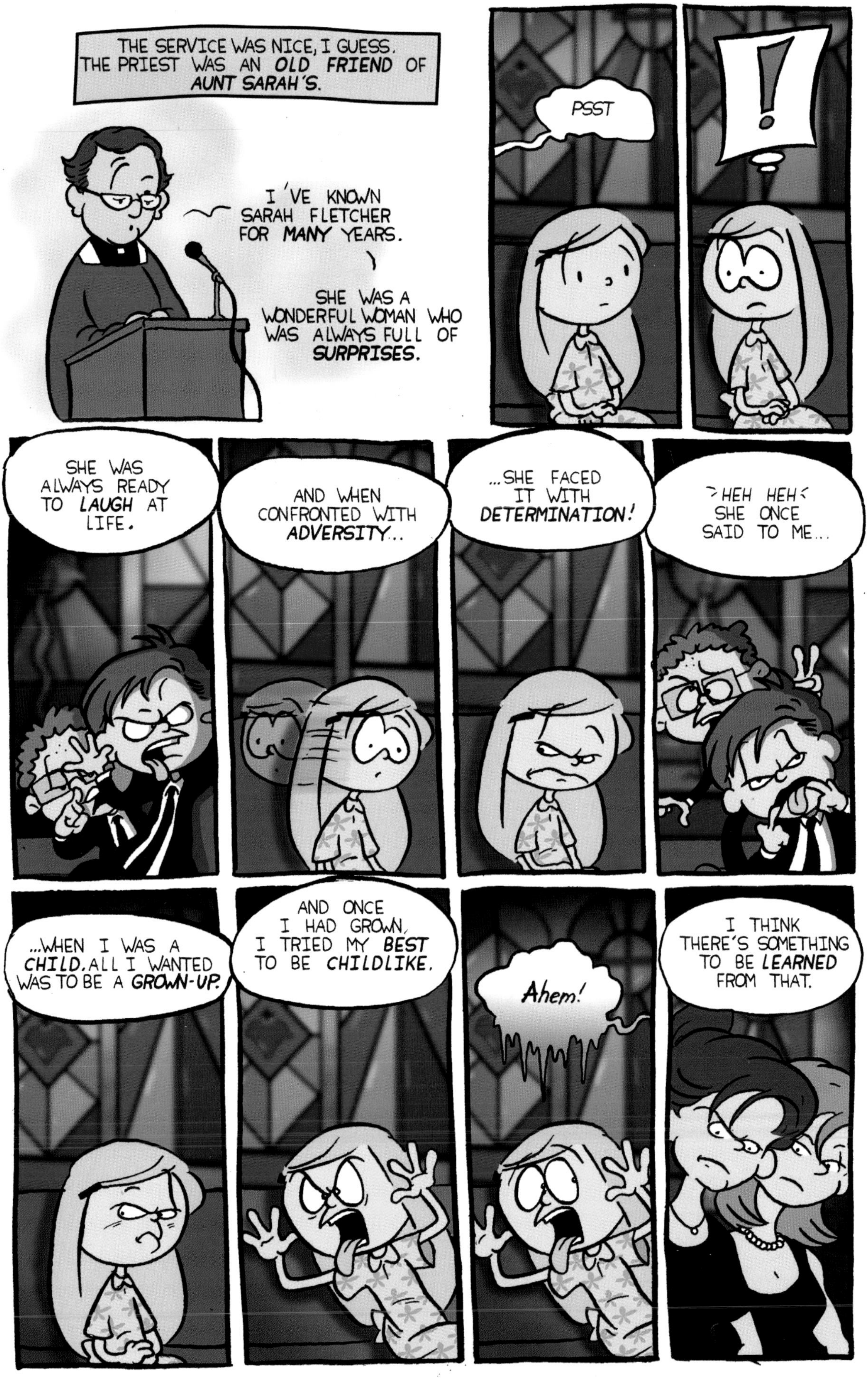
THE SERVICE WAS NICE, I GUESS. THE PRIEST WAS AN OLD FRIEND OF AUNT SARAH'S.
I'VE KNOWN SARAH FLETCHER FOR MANY YEARS.
SHE WAS A WONDERFUL WOMAN WHO WAS ALWAYS FULL OF SURPRISES.
PSST
!
SHE WAS ALWAYS READY TO LAUGH AT LIFE.
AND WHEN CONFRONTED WITH ADVERSITY...
...SHE FACED IT WITH DETERMINATION!
HEH HEH SHE ONCE SAID TO ME...
...WHEN I WAS A CHILD, ALL I WANTED WAS TO BE A GROWN-UP.
AND ONCE I HAD GROWN, I TRIED MY BEST TO BE CHILDLIKE.
Ahem!
I THINK THERE'S SOMETHING TO BE LEARNED FROM THAT.

AFTERWARD THERE WAS A RECEPTION AT THE HOUSE, BUT ALL I WANTED TO DO WAS GET **CHANGED** AND **GET AWAY.**

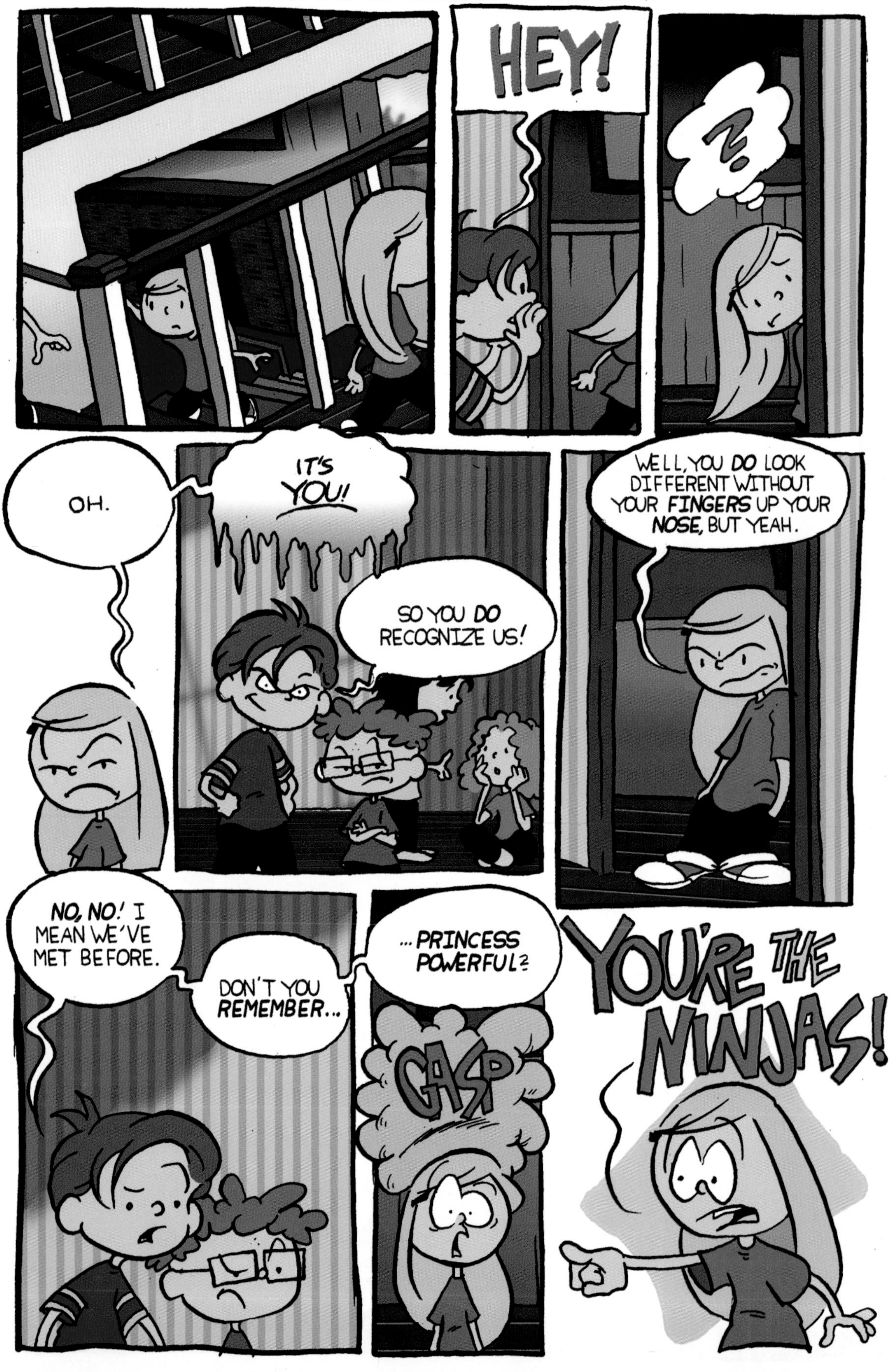

HEY!
?
OH.
IT'S YOU!
SO YOU DO RECOGNIZE US!
WELL, YOU DO LOOK DIFFERENT WITHOUT YOUR FINGERS UP YOUR NOSE, BUT YEAH.
NO, NO! I MEAN WE'VE MET BEFORE.
DON'T YOU REMEMBER...
...PRINCESS POWERFUL?
GASP
YOU'RE THE NINJAS!

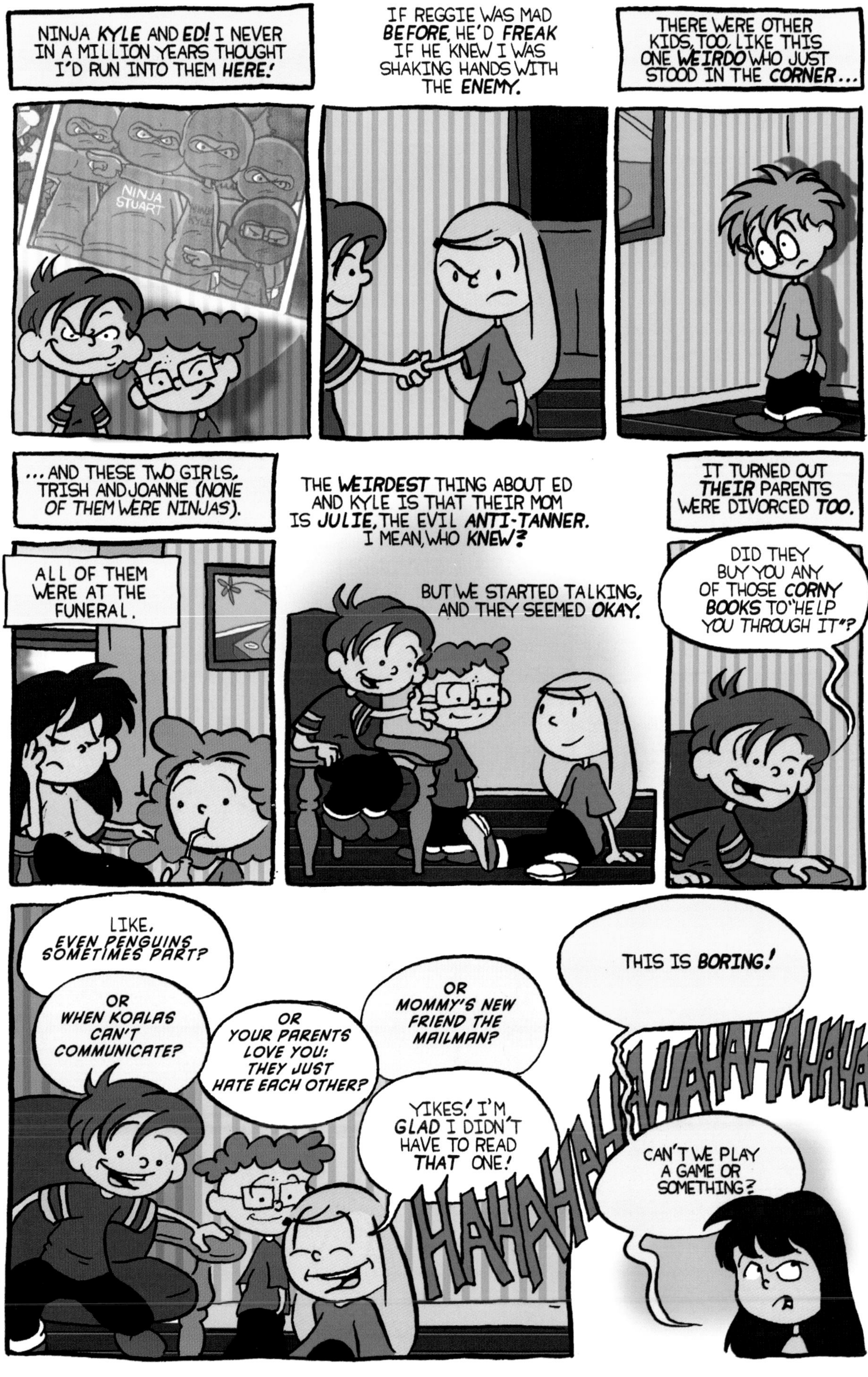
NINJA KYLE AND ED! I NEVER IN A MILLION YEARS THOUGHT I'D RUN INTO THEM HERE!
NINJA STUART
NINJA KYLE
IF REGGIE WAS MAD BEFORE, HE'D FREAK IF HE KNEW I WAS SHAKING HANDS WITH THE ENEMY.
THERE WERE OTHER KIDS, TOO, LIKE THIS ONE WEIRDO WHO JUST STOOD IN THE CORNER...
...AND THESE TWO GIRLS, TRISH AND JOANNE (NONE OF THEM WERE NINJAS).
ALL OF THEM WERE AT THE FUNERAL.
THE WEIRDEST THING ABOUT ED AND KYLE IS THAT THEIR MOM IS JULIE, THE EVIL ANTI-TANNER. I MEAN, WHO KNEW?
BUT WE STARTED TALKING, AND THEY SEEMED OKAY.
IT TURNED OUT THEIR PARENTS WERE DIVORCED TOO.
DID THEY BUY YOU ANY OF THOSE CORNY BOOKS TO "HELP YOU THROUGH IT"?
LIKE, EVEN PENGUINS SOMETIMES PART?
OR WHEN KOALAS CAN'T COMMUNICATE?
OR YOUR PARENTS LOVE YOU: THEY JUST HATE EACH OTHER?
OR MOMMY'S NEW FRIEND THE MAILMAN?
YIKES! I'M GLAD I DIDN'T HAVE TO READ THAT ONE!
HAHAHAHAHAHAHAHAHAHAHAHA
THIS IS BORING!
CAN'T WE PLAY A GAME OR SOMETHING?

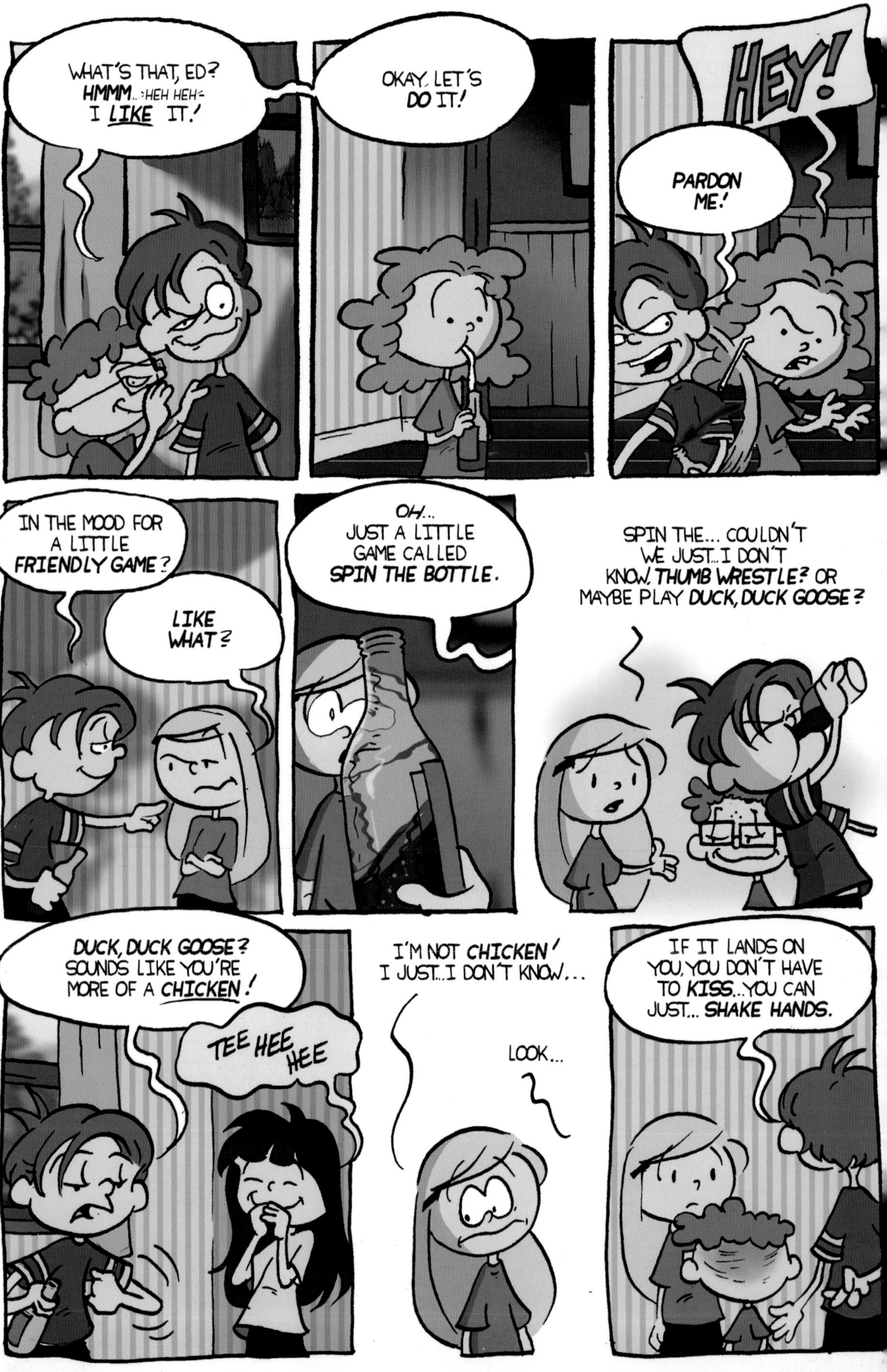
WHAT'S THAT, ED? HMMM... HEH HEH- I LIKE IT!
OKAY, LET'S DO IT!
HEY!
PARDON ME!
IN THE MOOD FOR A LITTLE FRIENDLY GAME?
LIKE WHAT?
OH... JUST A LITTLE GAME CALLED SPIN THE BOTTLE.
SPIN THE... COULDN'T WE JUST...I DON'T KNOW, THUMB WRESTLE? OR MAYBE PLAY DUCK, DUCK GOOSE?
DUCK, DUCK GOOSE? SOUNDS LIKE YOU'RE MORE OF A CHICKEN!
TEE HEE HEE
I'M NOT CHICKEN! I JUST...I DON'T KNOW...
LOOK...
IF IT LANDS ON YOU, YOU DON'T HAVE TO KISS...YOU CAN JUST... SHAKE HANDS.

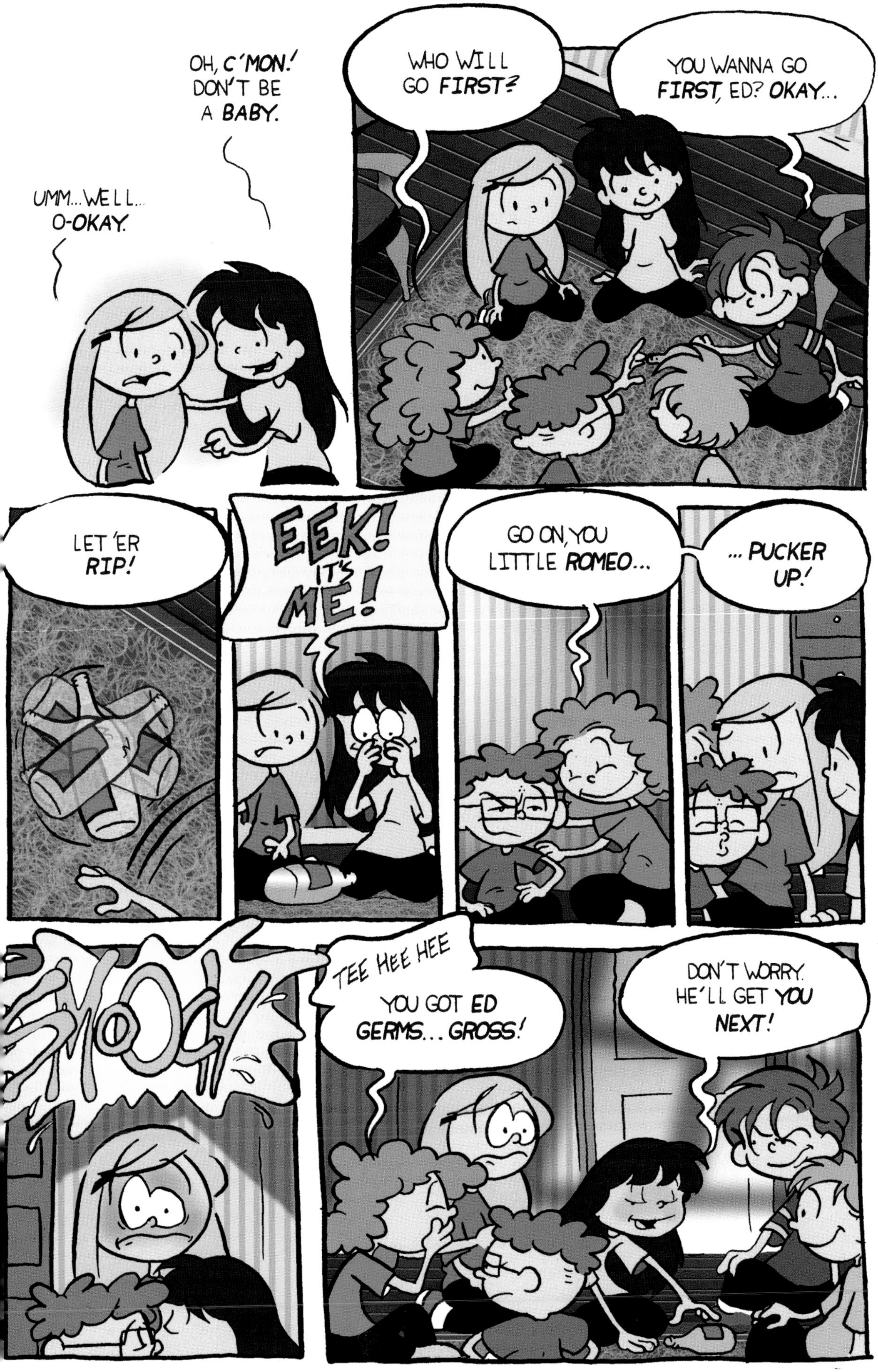
OH, C'MON! DON'T BE A BABY.
UMM... WELL... O-OKAY.
WHO WILL GO FIRST?
YOU WANNA GO FIRST, ED? OKAY...
LET 'ER RIP!
EEK! IT'S ME!
GO ON, YOU LITTLE ROMEO...
... PUCKER UP!
SMOOCH
TEE HEE HEE
YOU GOT ED GERMS... GROSS!
DON'T WORRY. HE'LL GET YOU NEXT!

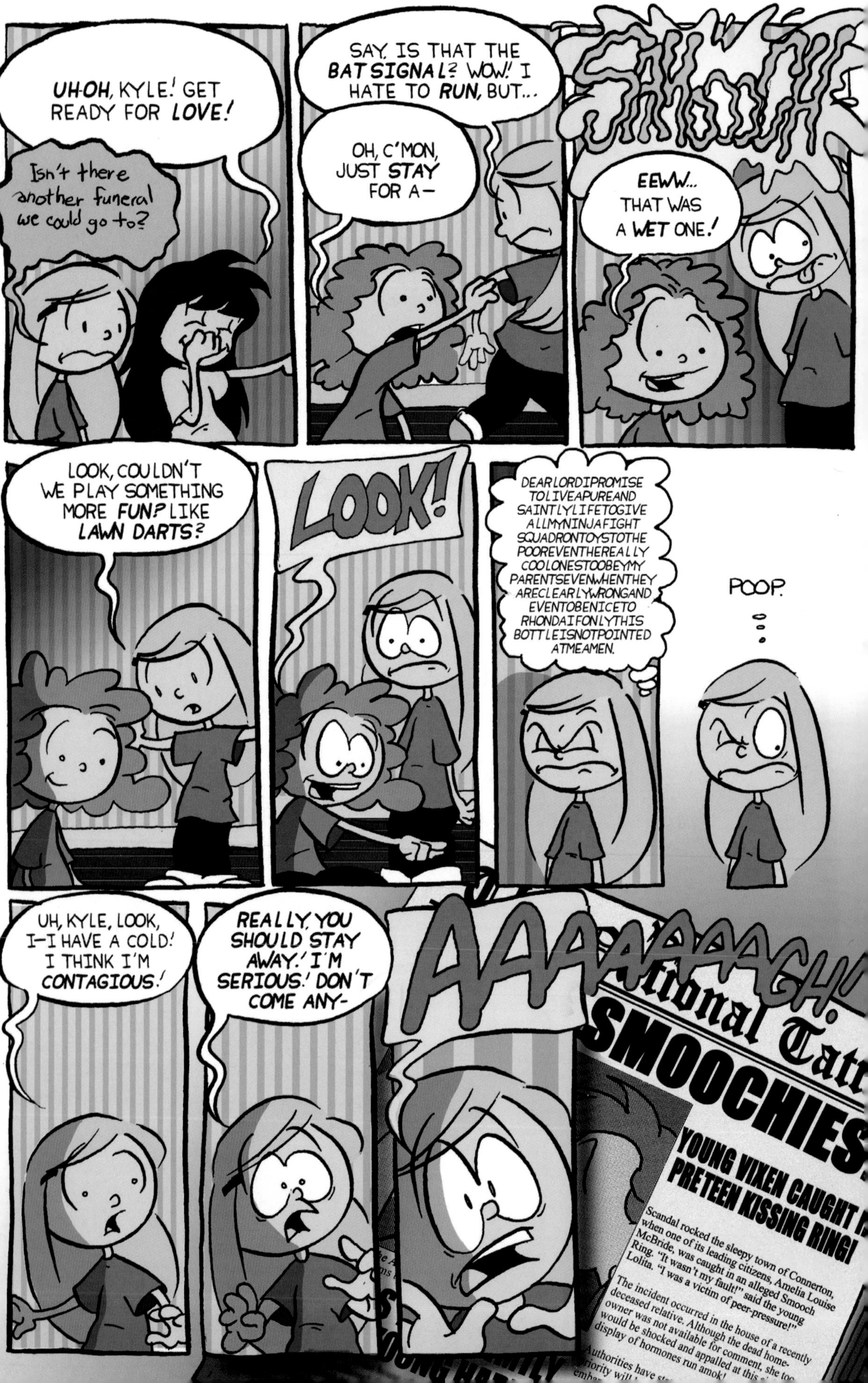
UH-OH, KYLE! GET READY FOR LOVE!
Isn't there another funeral we could go to?
SAY, IS THAT THE BAT SIGNAL? WOW! I HATE TO RUN, BUT...
OH, C'MON, JUST STAY FOR A—
SMOOCH
EEWW... THAT WAS A WET ONE!
LOOK, COULDN'T WE PLAY SOMETHING MORE FUN? LIKE LAWN DARTS?
LOOK!
DEARLORDIPROMISE TOLIVEAPUREAND SAINTLYLIFETOGIVE ALLMYNINJAFIGHT SQUADRONTOYSTOTHE POOREVENTHEREALLY COOLONESTOOBEYMY PARENTSEVENWHENTHEY ARECLEARLYWRONGAND EVENTOBENICETO RHONDAIFONLYTHIS BOTTLEISNOTPOINTED ATMEAMEN.
POOP.
UH, KYLE, LOOK, I—I HAVE A COLD! I THINK I'M CONTAGIOUS!
REALLY, YOU SHOULD STAY AWAY! I'M SERIOUS! DON'T COME ANY-
AAAAAAAGH!
SMOOCHIES
YOUNG VIXEN CAUGHT
PRETEEN KISSING RING!
Scandal rocked the sleepy town of Connerton, when one of its leading citizens, Amelia Louise McBride, was caught in an alleged Smooch Ring. "It wasn't my fault!" said the young Lolita. "I was a victim of peer-pressure!"
The incident occurred in the house of a recently deceased relative. Although the dead home-owner was not available for comment, she too would be shocked and appalled at this display of hormones run amok!

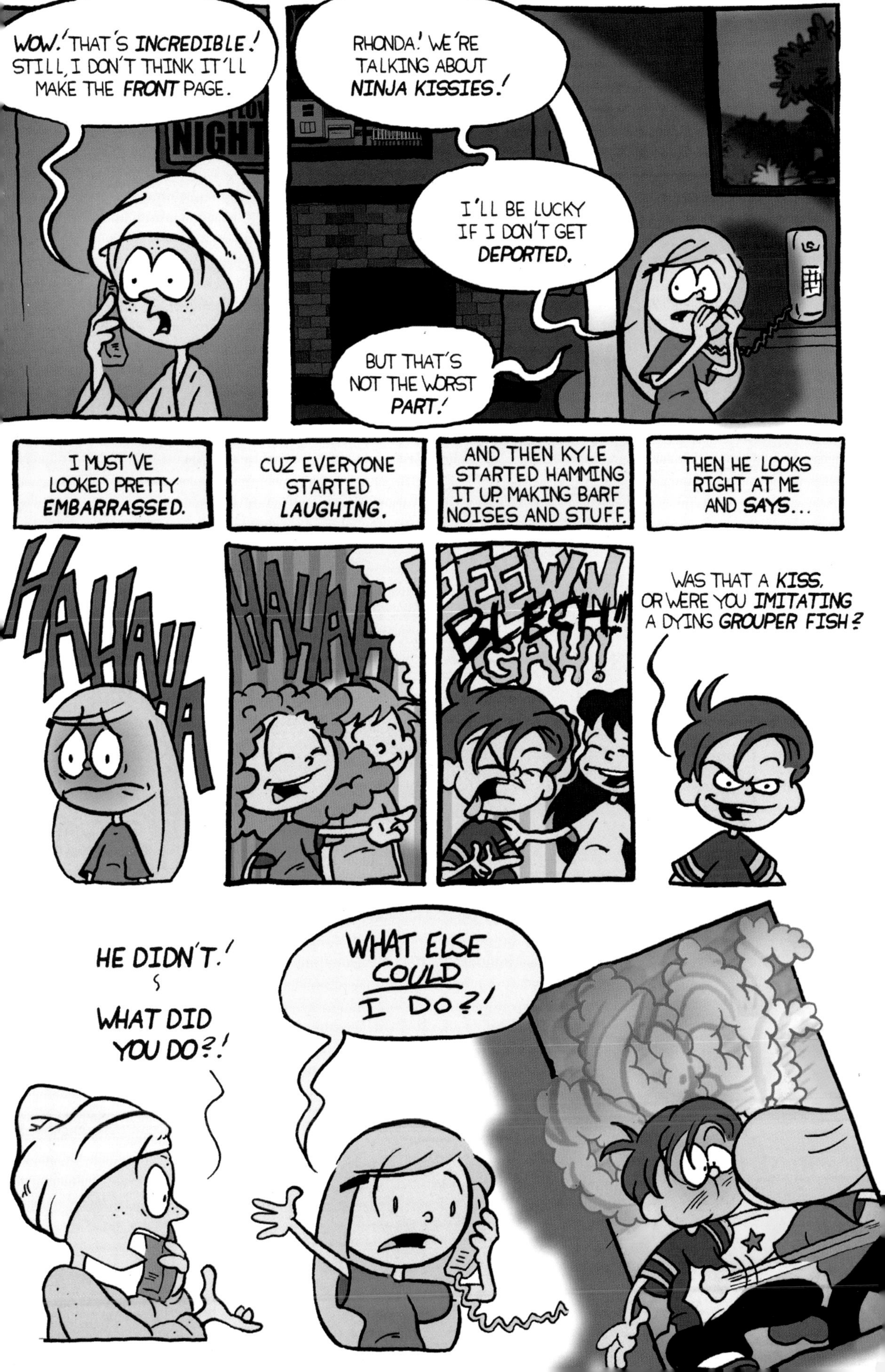
WOW! THAT'S INCREDIBLE! STILL, I DON'T THINK IT'LL MAKE THE FRONT PAGE.
RHONDA! WE'RE TALKING ABOUT NINJA KISSIES!
I'LL BE LUCKY IF I DON'T GET DEPORTED.
BUT THAT'S NOT THE WORST PART!
I MUST'VE LOOKED PRETTY EMBARRASSED.
CUZ EVERYONE STARTED LAUGHING.
AND THEN KYLE STARTED HAMMING IT UP. MAKING BARF NOISES AND STUFF.
THEN HE LOOKS RIGHT AT ME AND SAYS...
WAS THAT A KISS, OR WERE YOU IMITATING A DYING GROUPER FISH?
HE DIDN'T! WHAT DID YOU DO?!
WHAT ELSE COULD I DO?!

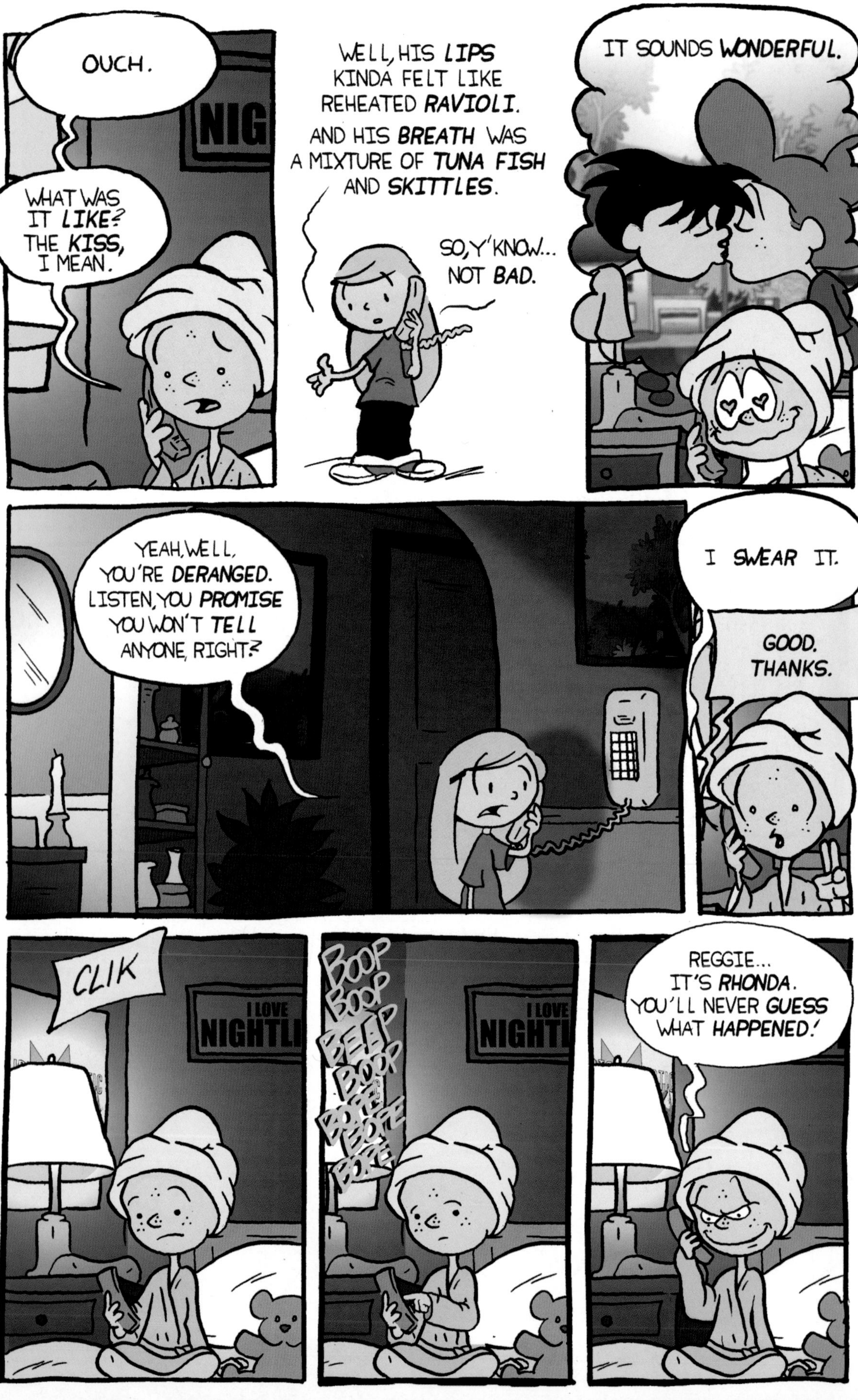

OUCH.
WHAT WAS IT LIKE? THE KISS, I MEAN.
WELL, HIS LIPS KINDA FELT LIKE REHEATED RAVIOLI.
AND HIS BREATH WAS A MIXTURE OF TUNA FISH AND SKITTLES.
SO, Y'KNOW... NOT BAD.
IT SOUNDS WONDERFUL.
YEAH, WELL, YOU'RE DERANGED. LISTEN, YOU PROMISE YOU WON'T TELL ANYONE, RIGHT?
I SWEAR IT.
GOOD. THANKS.
CLIK
BOOP
BOOP
REGGIE... IT'S RHONDA. YOU'LL NEVER GUESS WHAT HAPPENED!

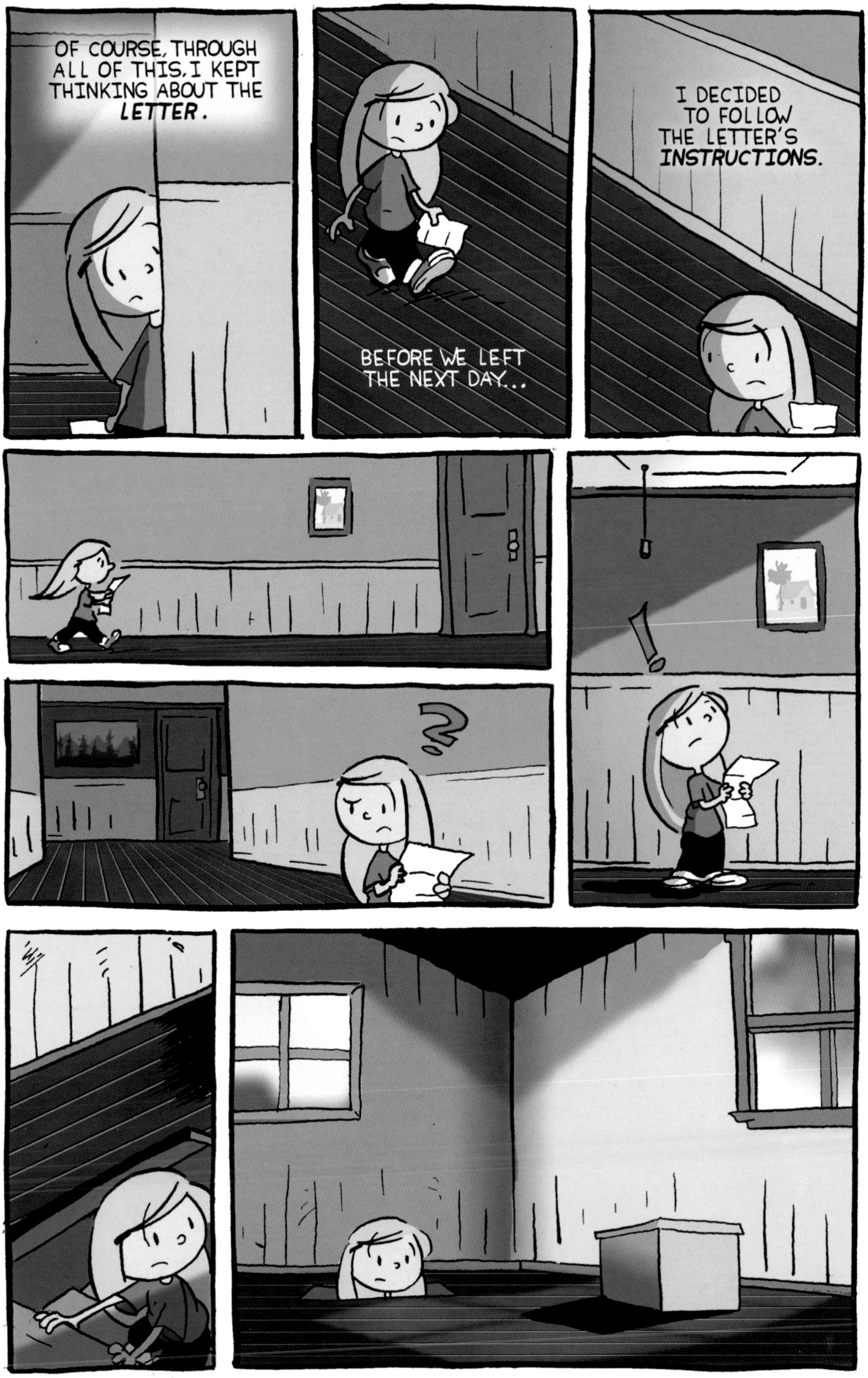

OF COURSE, THROUGH ALL OF THIS, I KEPT THINKING ABOUT THE LETTER.
BEFORE WE LEFT THE NEXT DAY...
I DECIDED TO FOLLOW THE LETTER'S INSTRUCTIONS.

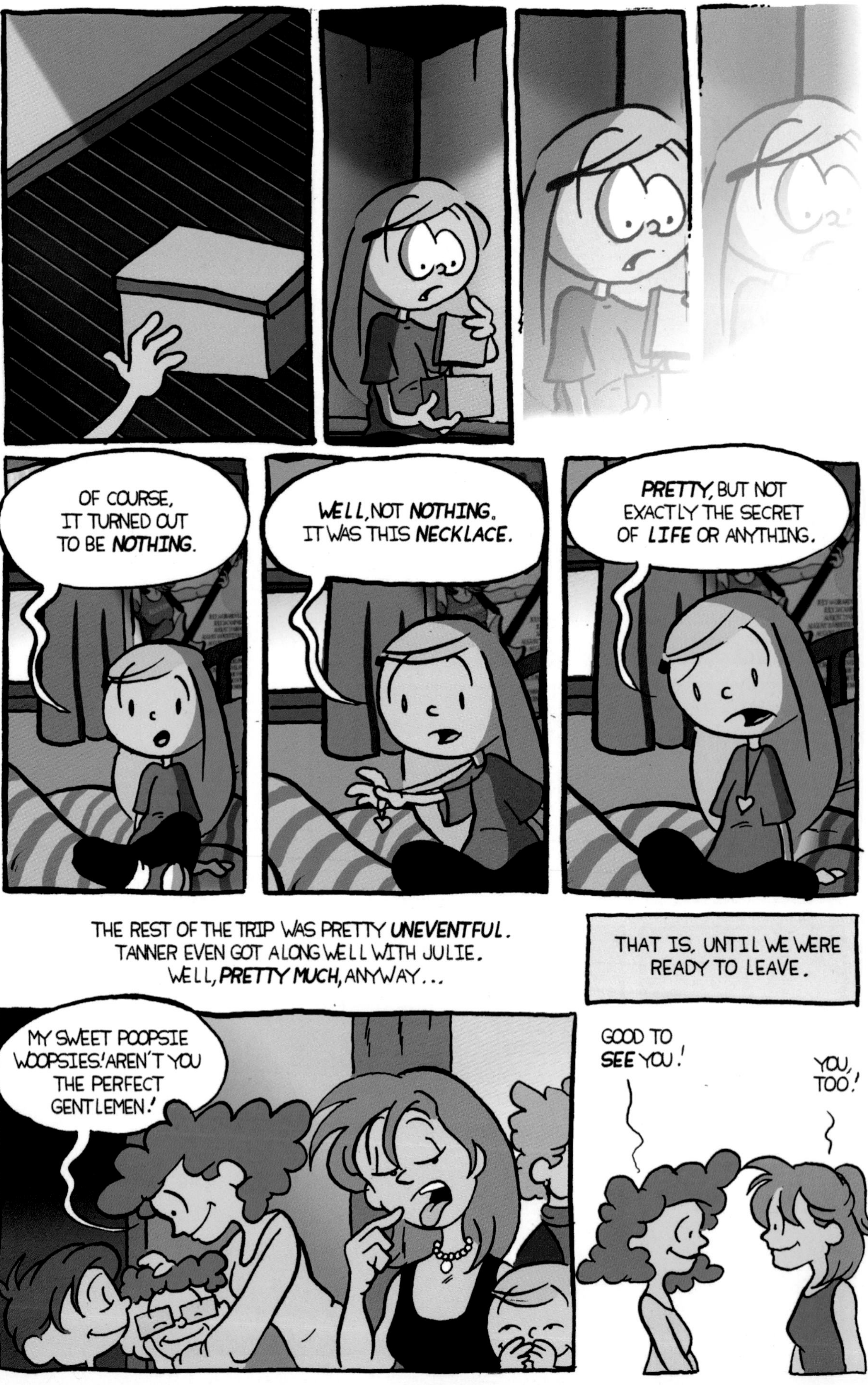
OF COURSE, IT TURNED OUT TO BE NOTHING.
WELL, NOT NOTHING. IT WAS THIS NECKLACE.
PRETTY, BUT NOT EXACTLY THE SECRET OF LIFE OR ANYTHING.
THE REST OF THE TRIP WAS PRETTY UNEVENTFUL. TANNER EVEN GOT ALONG WELL WITH JULIE. WELL, PRETTY MUCH, ANYWAY...
THAT IS, UNTIL WE WERE READY TO LEAVE.
MY SWEET POOPSIE WOOPSIES! AREN'T YOU THE PERFECT GENTLEMEN!
GOOD TO SEE YOU!
YOU, TOO!

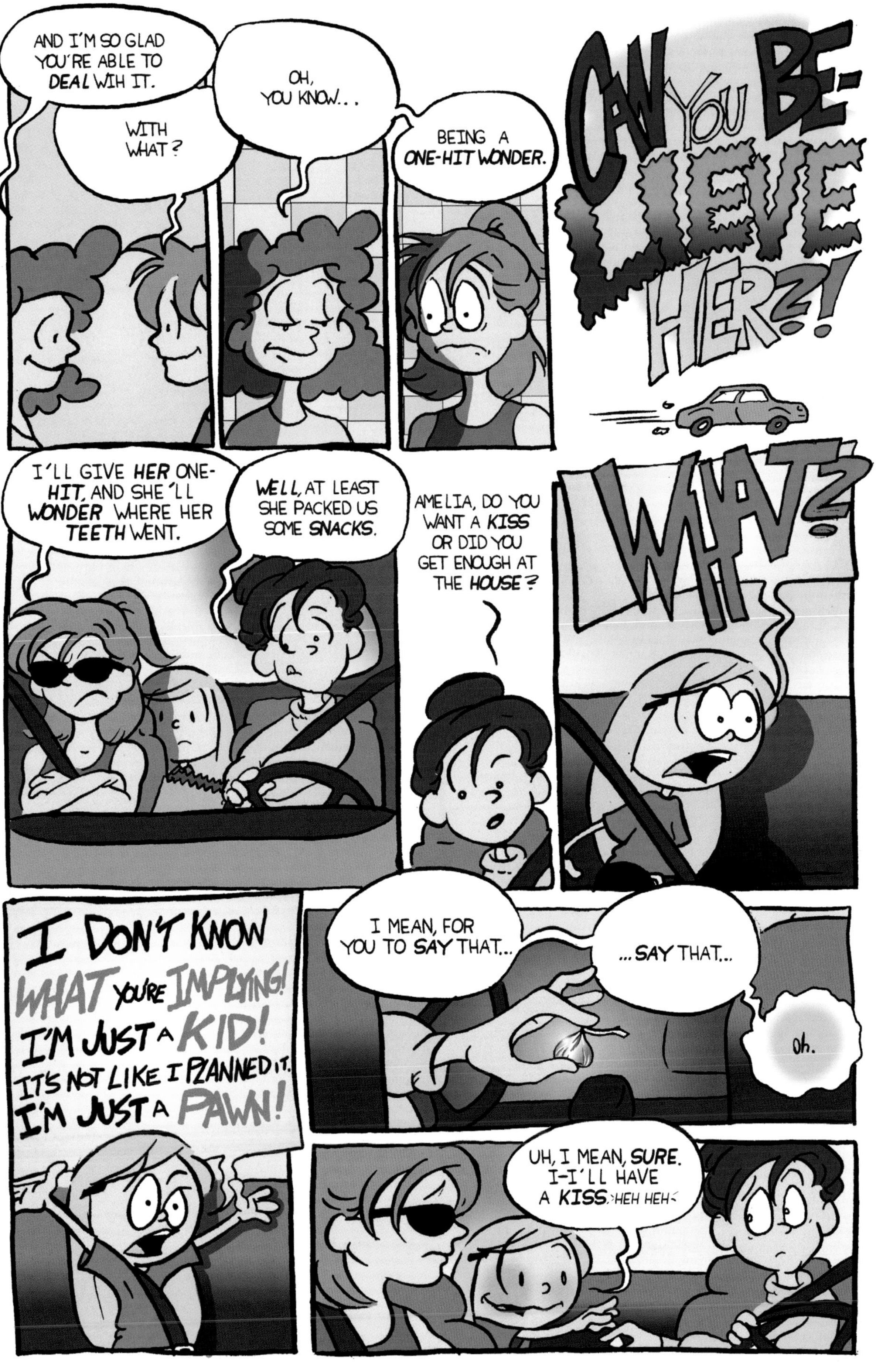
AND I'M SO GLAD YOU'RE ABLE TO DEAL WIH IT.
WITH WHAT?
OH, YOU KNOW. . .
BEING A ONE-HIT WONDER.
CAN YOU BE-LIEVE HER?!
I'LL GIVE HER ONE-HIT, AND SHE'LL WONDER WHERE HER TEETH WENT.
WELL, AT LEAST SHE PACKED US SOME SNACKS.
AMELIA, DO YOU WANT A KISS OR DID YOU GET ENOUGH AT THE HOUSE?
WHAT?
I DON'T KNOW WHAT YOU'RE IMPLYING! I'M JUST A KID! IT'S NOT LIKE I PLANNED IT. I'M JUST A PAWN!
I MEAN, FOR YOU TO SAY THAT...
...SAY THAT...
Oh.
UH, I MEAN, SURE. I-I'LL HAVE A KISS. >HEH HEH<

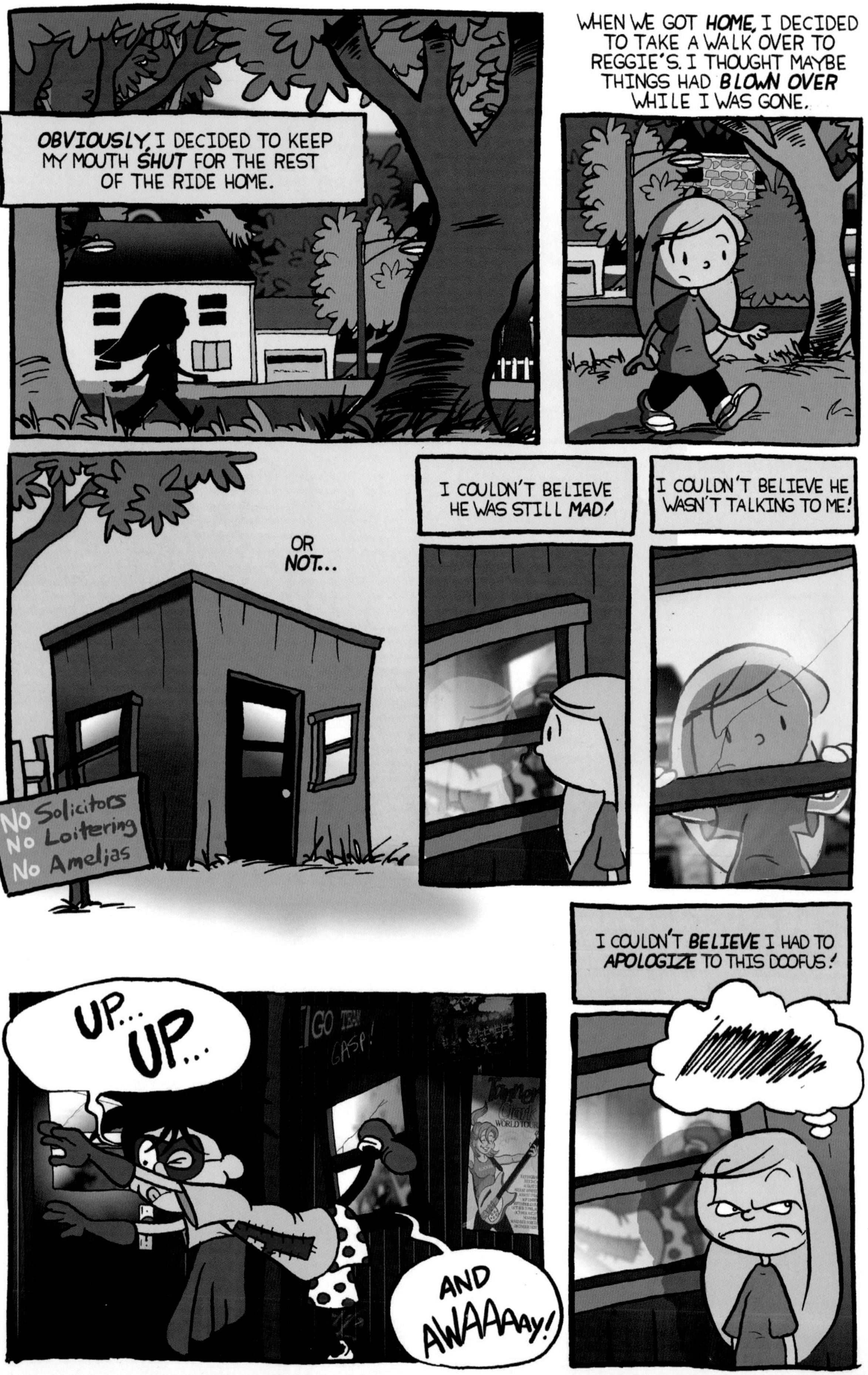
OBVIOUSLY, I DECIDED TO KEEP MY MOUTH SHUT FOR THE REST OF THE RIDE HOME.
WHEN WE GOT HOME, I DECIDED TO TAKE A WALK OVER TO REGGIE'S. I THOUGHT MAYBE THINGS HAD BLOWN OVER WHILE I WAS GONE.
OR NOT...
No Solicitors
No Loitering
No Amelias
I COULDN'T BELIEVE HE WAS STILL MAD!
I COULDN'T BELIEVE HE WASN'T TALKING TO ME!
UP... UP...
GO TEAM
GASP!
WORLD TOUR
AND AWAAAAay!
I COULDN'T BELIEVE I HAD TO APOLOGIZE TO THIS DOOFUS!

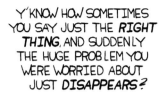

Y'KNOW HOW SOMETIMES YOU SAY JUST THE *RIGHT THING*, AND SUDDENLY THE HUGE PROBLEM YOU WERE WORRIED ABOUT JUST *DISAPPEARS*?

AND THE PERSON YOU WERE *FIGHTING* WITH IS REALLY *UNDERSTANDING* AND *SWEET*? AND THEY *TOTALLY* FORGIVE YOU?

WELL, THIS WASN'T LIKE THAT.

Mercy.

Uncle.

WHAT IS WRONG WITH YOU? JUST LEAVE ME ALONE!

GOOD-BYE.

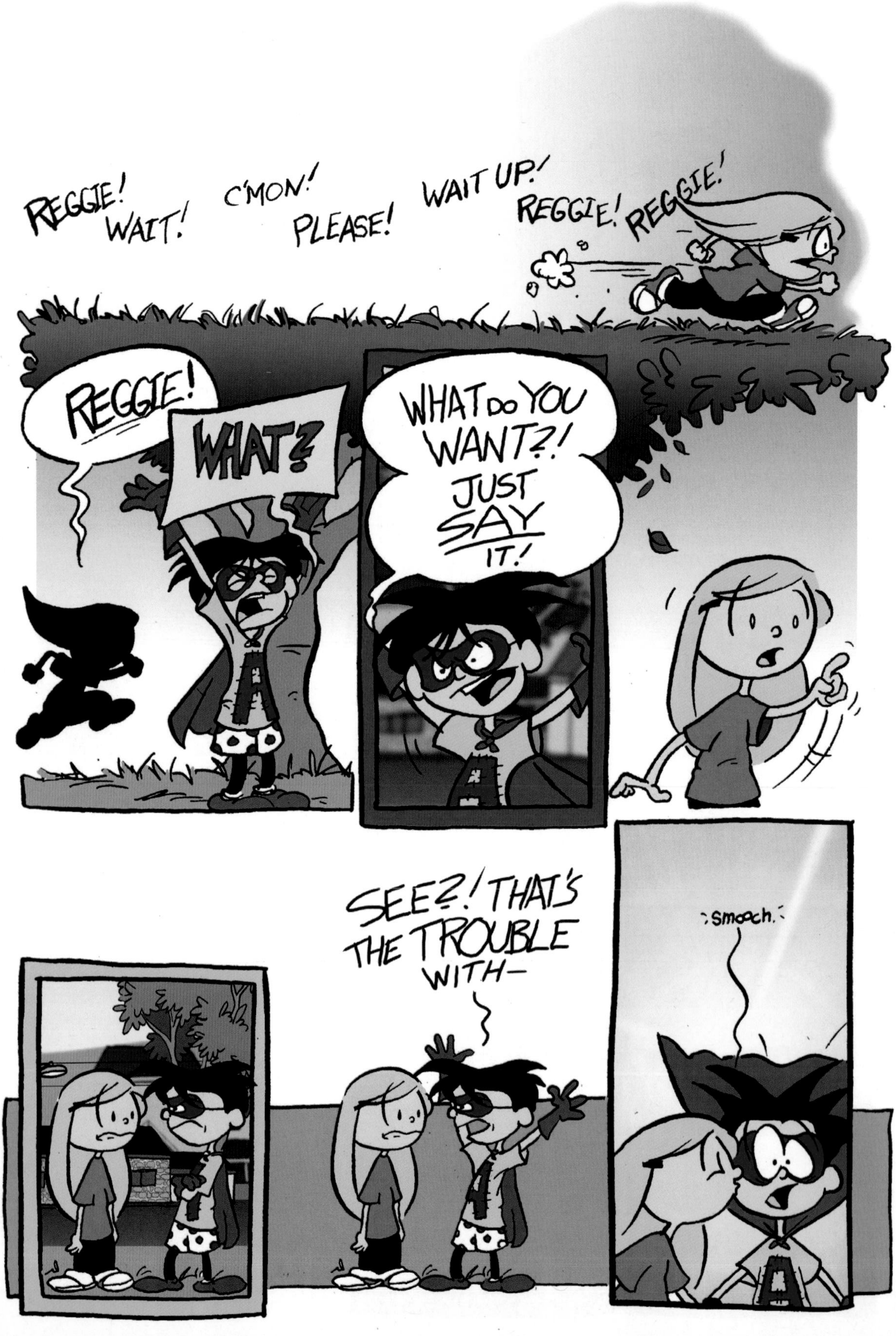
REGGIE! WAIT!
C'MON!
PLEASE!
WAIT UP!
REGGIE!
REGGIE!
REGGIE!
WHAT?
WHAT DO YOU WANT?! JUST SAY IT!
SEE?! THAT'S THE TROUBLE WITH-
smooch.

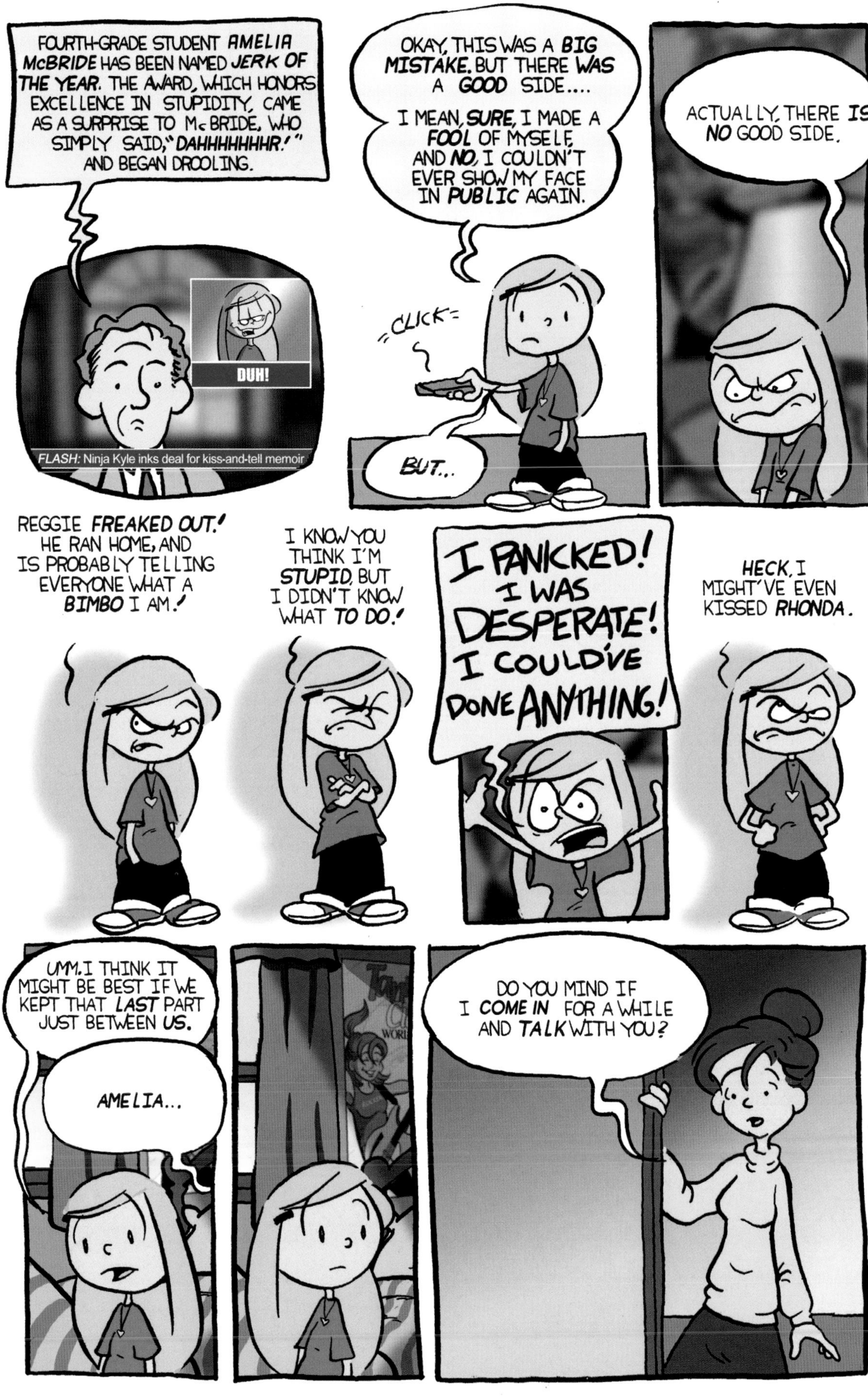
FOURTH-GRADE STUDENT AMELIA McBRIDE HAS BEEN NAMED JERK OF THE YEAR. THE AWARD, WHICH HONORS EXCELLENCE IN STUPIDITY, CAME AS A SURPRISE TO McBRIDE, WHO SIMPLY SAID, "DAHHHHHHHR!" AND BEGAN DROOLING.
DUH!
FLASH: Ninja Kyle inks deal for kiss-and-tell memoir
OKAY, THIS WAS A BIG MISTAKE. BUT THERE WAS A GOOD SIDE....
I MEAN, SURE, I MADE A FOOL OF MYSELF, AND NO, I COULDN'T EVER SHOW MY FACE IN PUBLIC AGAIN.
CLICK
BUT...
ACTUALLY, THERE IS NO GOOD SIDE.
REGGIE FREAKED OUT! HE RAN HOME, AND IS PROBABLY TELLING EVERYONE WHAT A BIMBO I AM!
I KNOW YOU THINK I'M STUPID, BUT I DIDN'T KNOW WHAT TO DO!
I PANICKED! I WAS DESPERATE! I COULD'VE DONE ANYTHING!
HECK, I MIGHT'VE EVEN KISSED RHONDA.
UMM. I THINK IT MIGHT BE BEST IF WE KEPT THAT LAST PART JUST BETWEEN US.
AMELIA...
DO YOU MIND IF I COME IN FOR A WHILE AND TALK WITH YOU?

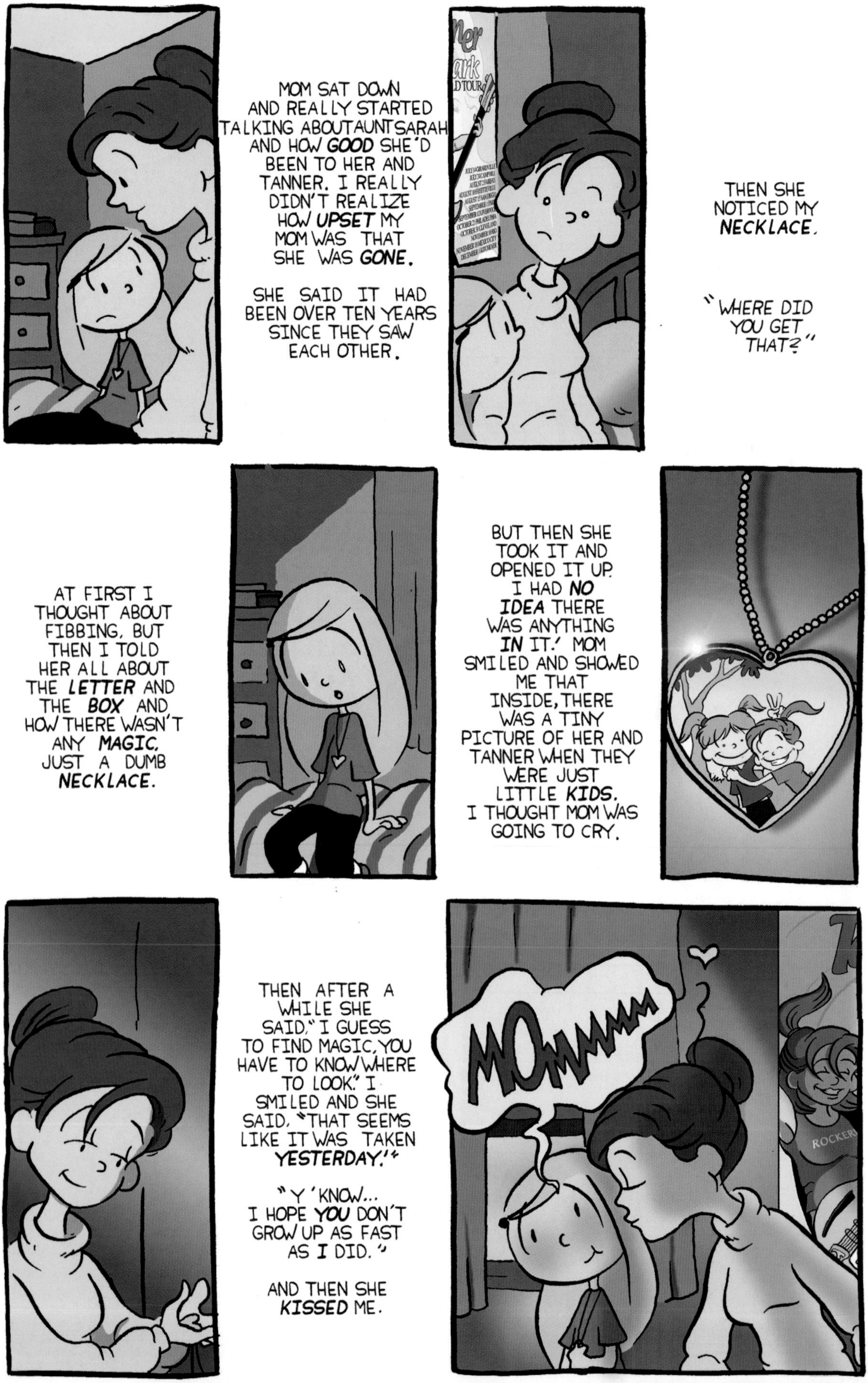
MOM SAT DOWN AND REALLY STARTED TALKING ABOUT AUNT SARAH AND HOW GOOD SHE'D BEEN TO HER AND TANNER. I REALLY DIDN'T REALIZE HOW UPSET MY MOM WAS THAT SHE WAS GONE.
SHE SAID IT HAD BEEN OVER TEN YEARS SINCE THEY SAW EACH OTHER.
THEN SHE NOTICED MY NECKLACE.
"WHERE DID YOU GET THAT?"
AT FIRST I THOUGHT ABOUT FIBBING, BUT THEN I TOLD HER ALL ABOUT THE LETTER AND THE BOX AND HOW THERE WASN'T ANY MAGIC, JUST A DUMB NECKLACE.
BUT THEN SHE TOOK IT AND OPENED IT UP. I HAD NO IDEA THERE WAS ANYTHING IN IT.' MOM SMILED AND SHOWED ME THAT INSIDE, THERE WAS A TINY PICTURE OF HER AND TANNER WHEN THEY WERE JUST LITTLE KIDS. I THOUGHT MOM WAS GOING TO CRY.
THEN AFTER A WHILE SHE SAID, "I GUESS TO FIND MAGIC, YOU HAVE TO KNOW WHERE TO LOOK." I SMILED AND SHE SAID, "THAT SEEMS LIKE IT WAS TAKEN YESTERDAY."
"Y'KNOW... I HOPE YOU DON'T GROW UP AS FAST AS I DID."
AND THEN SHE KISSED ME.
MOMMMMM

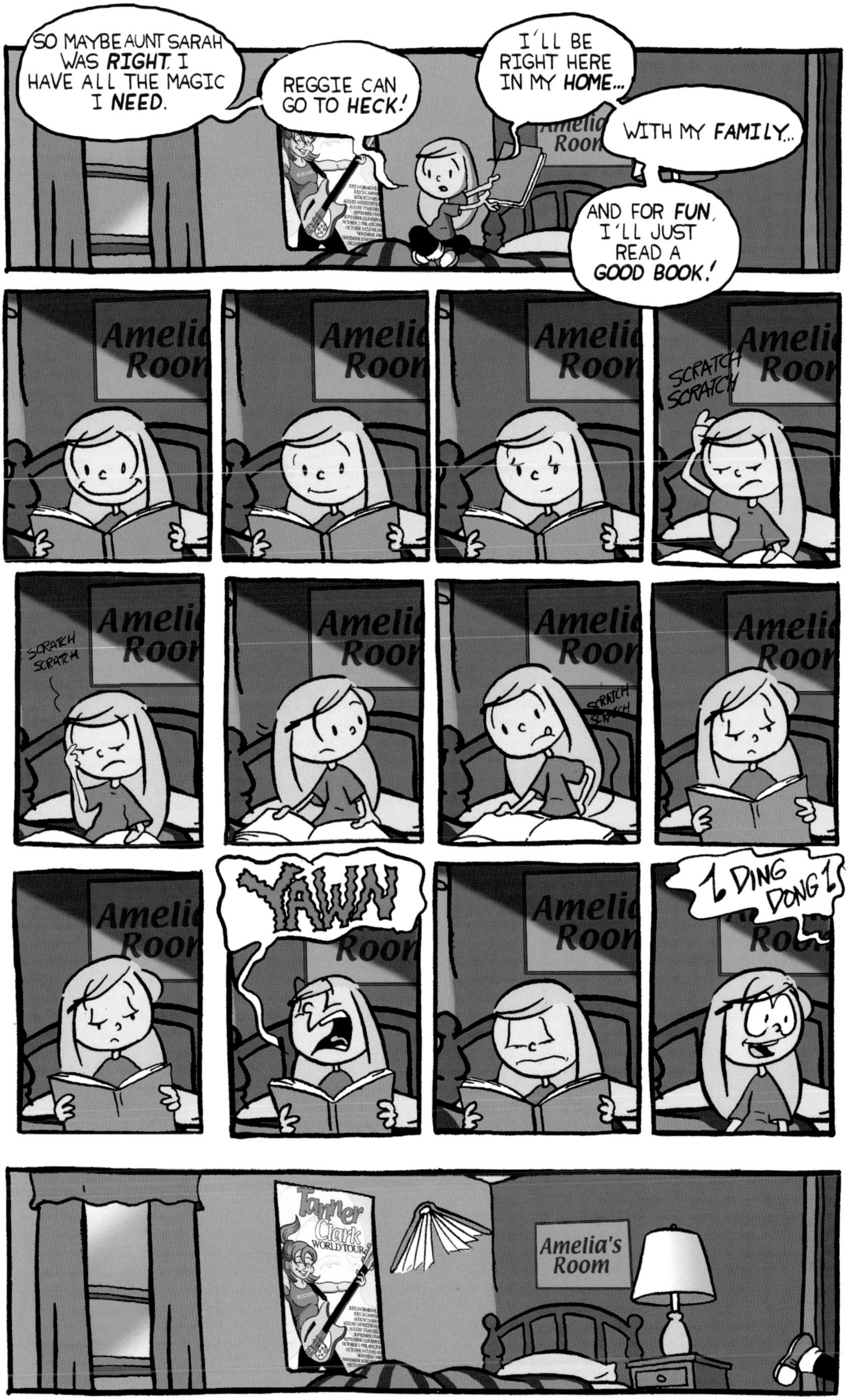
SO MAYBE AUNT SARAH WAS RIGHT. I HAVE ALL THE MAGIC I NEED.
REGGIE CAN GO TO HECK!
I'LL BE RIGHT HERE IN MY HOME...
WITH MY FAMILY...
AND FOR FUN, I'LL JUST READ A GOOD BOOK!
Amelia's Room
SCRATCH SCRATCH
SCRATCH SCRATCH
YAWN
DING DONG
Tanner Clark WORLD TOUR
Amelia's Room

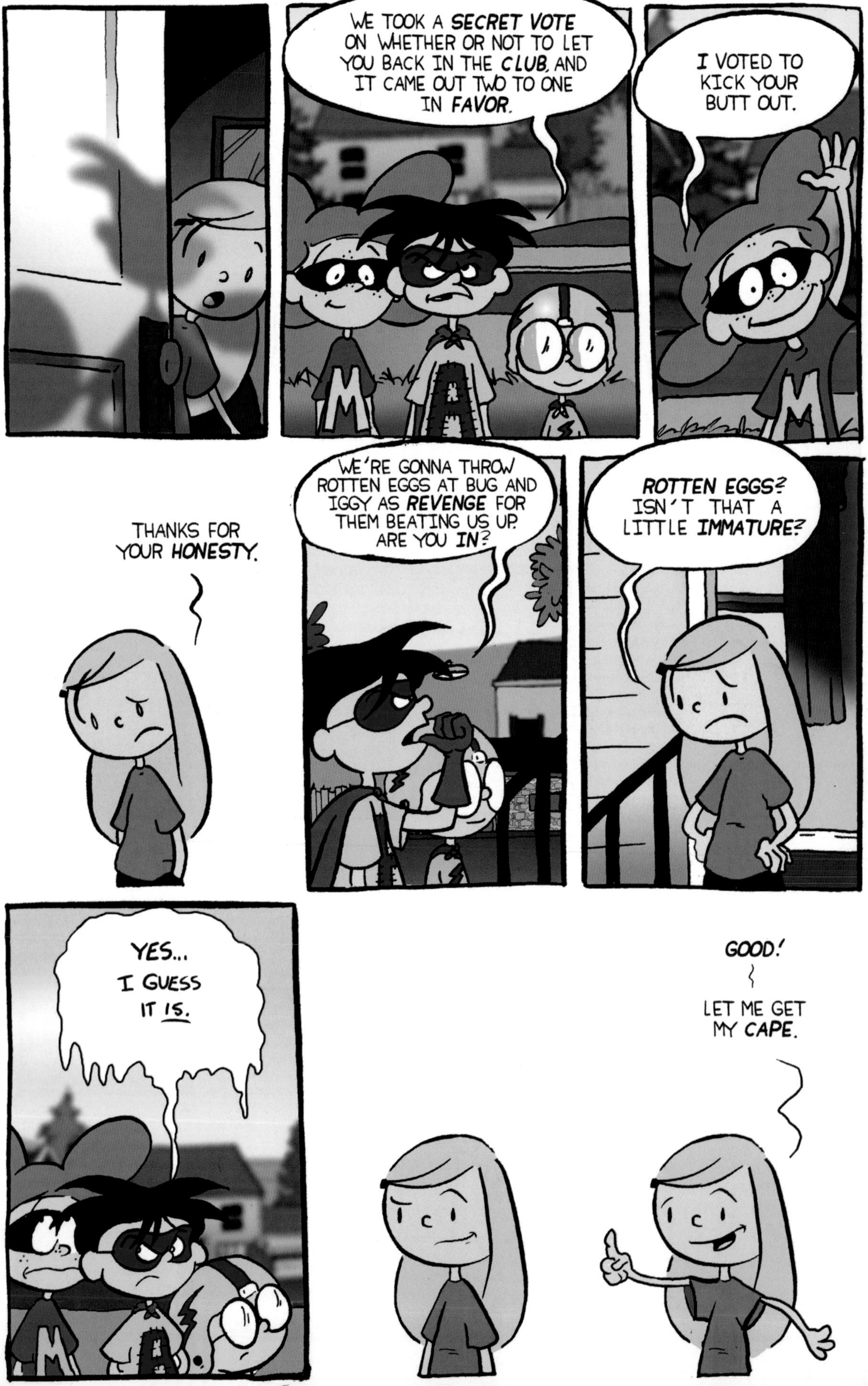
WE TOOK A SECRET VOTE ON WHETHER OR NOT TO LET YOU BACK IN THE CLUB, AND IT CAME OUT TWO TO ONE IN FAVOR.
I VOTED TO KICK YOUR BUTT OUT.
THANKS FOR YOUR HONESTY.
WE'RE GONNA THROW ROTTEN EGGS AT BUG AND IGGY AS REVENGE FOR THEM BEATING US UP. ARE YOU IN?
ROTTEN EGGS? ISN'T THAT A LITTLE IMMATURE?
YES... I GUESS IT IS.
GOOD!
LET ME GET MY CAPE.

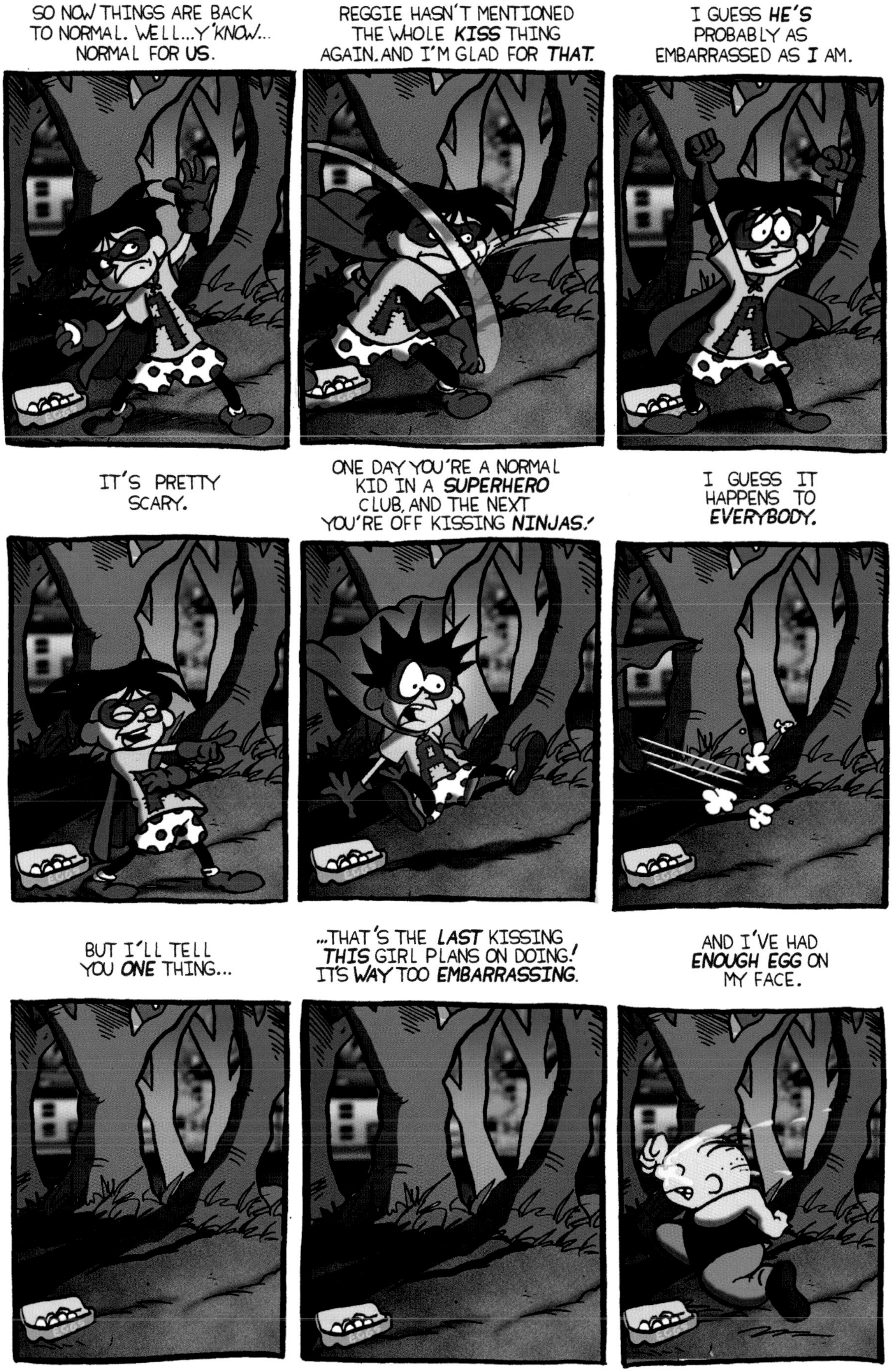
SO NOW THINGS ARE BACK TO NORMAL. WELL...Y'KNOW... NORMAL FOR US.
REGGIE HASN'T MENTIONED THE WHOLE KISS THING AGAIN. AND I'M GLAD FOR THAT.
I GUESS HE'S PROBABLY AS EMBARRASSED AS I AM.
IT'S PRETTY SCARY.
ONE DAY YOU'RE A NORMAL KID IN A SUPERHERO CLUB, AND THE NEXT YOU'RE OFF KISSING NINJAS!
I GUESS IT HAPPENS TO EVERYBODY.
BUT I'LL TELL YOU ONE THING...
...THAT'S THE LAST KISSING THIS GIRL PLANS ON DOING! IT'S WAY TOO EMBARRASSING.
AND I'VE HAD ENOUGH EGG ON MY FACE.

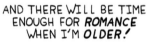

AND BESIDES, MOM IS PROBABLY **RIGHT**...

THERE'S NO POINT IN GROWING UP TOO **FAST**. I MEAN, WHO WANTS TO HAVE TO HAVE A **JOB**, OR A MORTGAGE, OR A 401K! HECK, I DON'T EVEN WANT TO KNOW WHAT A 401K **IS**!

AND THERE WILL BE TIME ENOUGH FOR **ROMANCE** WHEN I'M **OLDER**!

BUT BETWEEN YOU AND ME...

...I'M REALLY LOOKING **FORWARD** TO IT.